The Little Grey Girl

THE WILD MAGIC TRILOGY
BOOK 2

The *Little Grey Girl*

CELINE KIERNAN

CANDLEWICK PRESS

Text copyright © 2019 by Celine Kiernan
Illustrations copyright © 2019 by Jessica Courtney-Tickle

First US paperback edition 2021
First published by Walker Books (UK) 2019

Library of Congress Catalog Card Number 2019938949
ISBN 978-1-5362-0151-2 (hardcover)
ISBN 978-1-5362-1583-0 (paperback)

20 21 22 23 24 25 TRC 10 9 8 7 6 5 4 3 2 1

Printed in Eagan, MN, USA

This book was typeset in Joanna.
The illustrations were created digitally.

Candlewick Press
99 Dover Street
Somerville, Massachusetts 02144

www.candlewick.com

A JUNIOR LIBRARY GUILD SELECTION

For all the forgotten children

Over the Border to the Glittering Land

The old queen was not dead. That much was certain. No one knew where she was or how many of her witches were with her or what her plans might be — but everyone agreed that she could not be far away.

Some said she had become a storm cloud above Witches Borough, spying on everyone who spoke against her. Some said she hid behind the faces of ordinary animals, listening and watching and remembering.

Her defeat had been a trick, they said.

She was only testing them.

She would be back.

And when she returned, woe betide anyone foolish enough to have sided with her daughter.

* * *

Mam would not allow any of these rumours to stop her. In the weeks that followed the queen's defeat, she strode through all the doubts and fear with grave determination, coming and going across the border, carrying on with her plans. Finally it was time to move, and Mam came home one last time, ready to bring Mup and Dad and Tipper across the border. Ready to start their new life in the Glittering Land.

She had told Mup to bring her favourite things with her when she moved. "My mother's castle is a strange, cold place, Mup. If we are to live there, you should take some of your old life with you — to make things easier."

Mup chose her pink-and-yellow bed. She chose the writing desk and chair that Dad had made for her and that were painted with butterflies and flowers. She chose her bookcase and all her many books. She chose a mountain of multicoloured cushions and her wardrobe overflowing with rainbow-bright clothes.

That should be enough, she thought, staring at the colourful jumble piled in the frosty garden. *Enough things to fill a bedroom and make a place of my very own.*

But was it enough? Would any cushion be comfy enough to soften the cold rooms of the old queen's palace? Would any painted chair be bright enough to cancel out the darkness there?

Dad squeezed her shoulder and smiled his warm smile. "Come on, Mup. Lots to do."

He and Mup and Mam spent that whole morning staggering up and down the lawn, carrying all their things. They brought them through the dark trees at the end of their garden and down to the edge of the river, which Mup had once thought was just a stream, but which she now knew was the border to Witches Borough.

There was a raft floating there and they heaped their belongings onto it. The two steers-folk — natives of Witches Borough — leaned on their poles and eyed the growing pile as if the beds and chairs and books and blankets were the strangest things they'd ever seen.

Overhead, the branches rustled with sharp-eyed ravens. All around them the shadows flowed with watchful cats. Mup knew these were Clann'n Cheoil — the music people. She knew they were there to protect Mam and keep her safe. But on this side of the border the clann insisted on staying in their animal forms, and — ashamed as she was to admit it — Mup couldn't tell one of them from the other.

You could be anyone, she thought, eyeing each cat

and raven as she approached them. *You could even be a raggedy witch.*

Mup's newfound suspicion gave her friend Crow no end of grumpy amusement. But Mup wasn't willing to take any chances. Particularly when her little brother, Tipper, was still so young and her dog, Badger, was so old. Particularly when Dad hadn't a trace of magic with which to defend himself. (And as for Crow, he needed protecting too; no matter *how* loudly he protested otherwise.)

Just let someone try something, Mup thought. *Just let them try. Me and Mam will sort them out.* After everything that had happened, Mup was determined her family would never be hurt again.

At last, there was only Tipper's cot left to carry and all his baby things.

Mup helped Dad with them while Mam stood by the back door of their house, speaking with Fírinne, the leader of *Clann'n Cheoil.*

"People will never accept you as queen if you insist on lugging your own furniture about," grumbled Fírinne.

"I've told you before," said Mam. "I am not a queen."

Fírinne tutted in impatience. "If they can't bow to you, Stella, they'll look for someone else to bow to. You

4

need to take control. *Now*. While they're all still afraid of you."

Carrying Tipper's cot down the garden with Dad, Mup craned her neck to keep Fírinne in sight. The tall, silver-haired woman was the first friend Mup could ever remember Mam having. For all her talk of bowing, there was something fierce and proud and unbending about her. Mup liked her.

Mam gestured as if to assure her friend that she would be all right. With another tut, Fírinne stretched, transformed into a cat, and prowled grouchily off into the shadows.

Mam was left on her own, looking thoughtful.

She'll be OK, thought Mup with a twist of pride. *She's Mam. Nothing can hurt her.*

Down on the raft, Tipper was sitting to attention with Badger, ostentatiously guarding the heap of belongings. When Mup and Dad emerged into the sunshine, carrying his things, he barked excitedly.

"I don't needs any of them stuffs now, Daddy!" he barked. "Remember? I'm's a dog!"

Dad chuckled and bent from his great height to scratch his son between his ears. "You never know what you might want to be, Tip. Don't limit your possibilities."

Mup stood back, surveying their belongings. "I . . . I think that's it, Dad," she said.

Dad crouched in front of Tipper. "Tip, won't you come up and say goodbye to our house?"

Tipper backed away. He knew that as soon as he stepped off the raft, he'd turn back into a human baby. Tipper very much did not want to be a human baby.

Dad glanced up at Mup. She shrugged.

"You sure, Tip?" she asked. "Daddy can carry you."

But Tipper just retreated to lie at Badger's side. He rested his golden head on his big golden paws. "Me'll wait here," he said softly.

Mam and Dad talked in the kitchen while Mup walked from room to room saying goodbye.

The house was unnaturally quiet and still. Already, it seemed to be gathering dust.

There came a flutter of shadow, and a glossy young raven flew in at the door. It hopped across the floor to her, shook itself in a disgruntled manner, and transformed into the thin, wild-haired boy Mup now thought of as her best friend: Crow.

Crow frowned at the expression on Mup's face.

> "Why the frown so grim and dreary,
> Have you decided not to leave?

Does crossing borders make you weary?

Will moving homes cause you to grieve?"

Mup smiled and, for what felt like the millionth time, said, "You don't have to speak in rhyme anymore, Crow. The old queen is gone and so are her horrible rules."

Crow just looked at her in his sideways fashion. "Are you not going to cross?" he said.

Mup looked around the house.

Crow has the clothes he wears, she thought. *That's all he owns in the world.*

She pulled on her rabbit-eared hat and firmly zipped up her red jacket. "Of course I'm crossing, Crow."

Together they walked out of the house and down to the river without looking back.

Within the shade of the pine trees, the ravens and cats kept guard and Mup and Crow watched the water, waiting for Mam and Dad to catch up. The far bank was hidden in light-dazzle. Nothing would become visible there until they crossed the border into Witches Borough. On this side of the river was Mup's normal life. On the other lay her grandmother's kingdom of witches, magic, war, strangeness.

"Are you scared, Mup?" asked Crow.

7

"Me's not scared!" barked Tipper from his perch on the raft. "Dogs are brave! Not like babies!"

I'm a bit scared, thought Mup.

But then again I am the hare — I am the stitcher of worlds.

She crouched and pressed her hand to the ground.

Show me, she thought.

The world immediately unfurled itself into a web of shining, silver paths visible only to her. Mup let her mind follow one of these paths down between the roots and stones of the riverbank, out beneath the cool water, across the weedy riverbed and over to the far side: to the Glittering Land, to Witches Borough, a place separate from the mundane world but part of it — a place the same and not the same all at once.

No need to be afraid, thought Mup. *Everything in the world is connected, and I am part of that. No matter where I go, I belong.*

Just then, Dad came through the trees. "Oops-a-daisy!" he yelled as he grabbed Mup under the arms and swung her out across the sunshine and onto the bobbing raft. Before she had time to find her footing, Dad picked up Crow and tossed him after her.

"I . . . I can fly, you know!" blustered Crow. "I don't need anyone to fling me!" And as if to prove it, he shook himself into his bird form and retreated in a disgruntled flurry of wings to the top of the belongings pile.

Mup grinned up at him from the deck.

"Sorry, Crow," called Dad cheerfully. "Not yet used to kids with wings!" He stepped across, his great size momentarily tilting the raft.

"Majesty," he teased, offering his hand to Mam, who was standing on the shore.

She just tutted fondly and lightly leapt on board.

Tipper bounced around her. "I looked-ed after all the things!" he barked. "Amn't I good?"

"You're very good," said Dad, hunkering down to scratch Tipper's ears. "A very good boy."

Mam smiled gravely.

Mup clapped her hands, suddenly delighted. Because what more did she need than this? Her and Crow, Tipper and Badger, Mam and Dad—all here in the brittle sunshine, ready to face things together. "Let's go!" she cried.

"Right-oh," said the steers-folk, and they pushed sharply from the shore.

The raft jolted. Everyone stumbled. The world spun upside down.

Mup's eyes and nose and mouth filled with the burbling river.

I remember this! she thought. *This upside-down, under-the-water, churny feeling!*

Fírinne had told her to trust the steers-folk. "They'll

9

get us where we need to go," she'd said. "Without them, we could end up scattered along the border, and I don't fancy hunting the countryside, hoping to find you before what's left of your grandmother's creatures do."

Trust the steers-folk, thought Mup as bubbles sang past her face and eyes. *Trust them.*

She clenched her hands against the urge to swim and grinned into the rushing torrent.

This was fun!

For a moment, there were little silver fish staring right into her face. They had to swim very fast to keep up with Mup's speedy pace.

Ooooooo, they sang. *The hare! The hare! We remember you!*

"Hello!" cried Mup, her breath a gurgle of bubbles. "It's nice to see you again!"

She quickly left the fishes behind, zooming ahead of them at tremendous speed. This journey was far more directed, far less chaotic than the first time she'd crossed the river.

Then the raft abruptly righted itself, the light cleared, and they were above the surface again.

Mam's hand was strong on Mup's shoulder. Dad and Tipper were sputtering and gasping. Crow shook invisible water from his wings. The steers-folk looked at them all as if they were half-baked in the brain-pan and commenced pushing their poles through the placid mirror of the wide river they now found themselves on.

We're here, thought Mup in excitement. *We're back in Witches Borough.*

The air was golden on this side of the border, and shimmering with the colours of autumn. On either side of the river, graceful trees shed leaves into the gently moving water. Overhead, the sky was purest blue.

As Mup took in all this astonishing colour, a huge flock of ravens burst from nowhere, cawing. The breeze from the birds' wings ruffled Mup's hat as they passed overhead, then they sailed onwards, their silhouettes reflected sharply in the river. In the dappled shadows of the riverbanks, numerous cats slunk into view, keeping pace with the raft.

Fírinne, thought Mup. *And the rest of the clann. They followed us.*

She turned to Dad. He stared all around him, frowning and wary. Mup took his hand. "Don't you remember anything about your first visit, Dad?"

He shook his head. "Do you?"

Mup nodded. *I remember everything.*

At the top of the belongings pile, Crow softly clacked his beak as if he too was remembering.

11

Mam went to stand at the head of the raft. Her hands deep in the pockets of her sensible coat, she watched the river unspool before her. "How much further to the castle?" she asked.

"Not far," answered the steers-folk. And though that shouldn't have been possible, Mup knew they were telling the truth.

Her grandmother's castle.

The very mention of it made her shiver. So many terrible things had happened there. Mup wasn't at all sure how she felt about it being her new home. *But things are different now.* She looked around at the ravens and the cats that followed and surrounded them. She flexed her hands, feeling the comforting tingle of magic at her fingertips. *We're making things different.*

"We're here," said Mam.

Already? Mup spun to look ahead. To her amazement, the square, blank walls of the castle were visible above the trees.

With a squawk, Crow skittered down the precarious jumble of belongings and over to Mup's shoulder. He perched there, close to her ear, the two of them gazing tensely upwards.

It's as if the castle was waiting on us, Mup thought. *As if . . .* She shivered again. *As if it's rushing us back into its arms.*

12

"We comed here in a cage, Daddy," whispered Tipper. "They putted us in the dark."

Dad laid a big comforting hand on Tipper's back, his dark eyes searching the turrets and towers, taking in the vast stone bulk of the place.

The steers-folk ceased poling, reluctant to get any closer. The raft, however, seemed to have other ideas, and it sailed smoothly onwards as if drawn in by the castle itself. They rounded the corner and it rose before them, its great, pale, silent reflection stretching across the motionless water. The walls seemed to grow taller as the raft passed into their shadow. Soon all on board had to strain their necks to look up.

The raft bumped the steps that led up the side of the castle. Mup remembered these steps lined with raggedy witches. She remembered the cold, pale faces, the cold, pale hands—the emotionless way they'd pulled the cage in. There had been a door at the top of the steps back then, but now a jagged hole punctured the once impregnable wall. Mam had torn this hole herself, during the battle to defeat Mup's grandmother. She had pulled the blocks down using her own wild magic and the powerful voices of *Clann'n Cheoil*.

"Wow," breathed Dad, staring upwards. "That's . . . that's some structure."

Mam glanced back at him, then up again to the gap in the wall. Figures were gathering there, staring down. Mam took a breath, stepped off the raft, and climbed the steps towards them. Overhead, her raven guards settled on the broken teeth of the walls. From the distant banks, cats swam towards her through the leaf-strewn water.

Far above, Mam reached the top and stepped from sight. Mup led the others up the stairs after her, Crow huddled on her shoulder, quietly chattering his beak.

The courtyard was filled with people: Clann'n Cheoil, Speirling, some villagers, some river people, a knot of wary castle staff. At the back of the rubble-strewn court-yard, at the base of one of the many staircases that led up and up to distant doors and windows, the small group of raggedy witches who had broken with the old queen stood isolated and aloof. At the sight of them, Crow bristled, his sharp feet biting into Mup's shoulder. Mup clenched her fists.

They said they were on Mam's side because she was stronger than the old queen. But how could they be trusted? Mup didn't like how confident they looked — despite their queen having been defeated in battle only weeks before. She didn't like how coldly they sneered at the people around them.

They still believe this is their home, she thought.

Well, they were wrong.

This was Mup's home now. Mup's and Dad's and Tipper's and Crow's.

There was no place here for the kind of cruelty these creatures were used to inflicting.

Mam would show them. Mam would make them see.

Mam hesitated a few paces into the courtyard, obviously daunted by the size of the crowd. She knew none of these people. All of them knew Mam, though, or at least knew of her. She was the stolen heir come home at last. They'd feared her mother, the old queen; they'd been abandoned by her aunty, the old queen's sister—and they'd finally had their hopes granted when Mam returned from nowhere to free them from her mother's tyranny.

But now what?

The crowd regarded Mam with wariness. Not sure, Mup supposed, what to make of her or where things might go from here. In the watchful quiet, she went to Mam's side.

Behind them, Dad was leading Tipper and Badger up the stairs. Tipper was pressed to Dad's legs, his eyes roaming the walls and the sky and the people. Badger was panting with the effort of the climb. Before they could reach the top step, Fírinne came striding up behind them and pushed her way past.

Her silver hair flying, her face set in grim determination, the tall woman shoved Mup aside. She grabbed Mam's hand and flung it aloft in a gesture of proud defiance.

"Behold!" she yelled. "Your new queen!"

Mam gasped, No.

The crowd, their faces suddenly luminous with relief, went wild. A queen, it would appear, was something they all knew how to deal with. Instantly, they began pulling papers from their pockets. Instantly, they began elbowing each other aside. Mup noticed that the stiffly dressed castle folk—the Speirling and the old queen's remaining staff—were the ones to most eagerly push forward.

"Majesty!" they cried, their hands extended, the papers fluttering. "Majesty! Hear me!" Watched by the cool, pale-faced witches and a fiercely triumphant Fírinne, the crowd surged towards Mam in a great roaring wave of urgency.

Dad pulled Tipper to him in alarm. "Let's get the kids inside!" he shouted.

Mam was busy yelling at Fírinne. "We agreed, Fírinne! I will not be a queen . . ."

The crowd closed in. Mup staggered backwards, people on all sides. A man leaned over her, waving papers, the huge lace ruff at his neck blocking the light. Crow squawked as he was knocked from Mup's shoulder. Mup tripped over someone's legs. She tumbled between close-pressed bodies and slammed to her hands and knees in a stamping chaos of feet.

"Majesty!" yelled a voice overhead. "A petition! A petition!"

The shouter's buckled shoes missed Mup's fingers by a fraction.

"Get back!" she cried, elbowing him in the kneecaps.

"Majesty, are Clann'n Cheoil your enforcers?"

This person accidentally kicked Crow, who rolled away in an outraged fluff of feathers.

"Hey!" Mup yelled, squeezing through legs to get to him. "Hey! That's my friend!"

She grabbed Crow and clung to him in the tumult.

"Majesty, shall you kill the old queen?"

Mup zapped this person: a little jolt to send them hopping.

"Majesty, may we speak in private?"

Mup slapped this person with her hat. But it was getting dark and frightening. It was getting hard to breathe. All was crushing, crowding legs and heedless adults pushing forward.

"Stop!" she yelled desperately. *"Stop!"*

Then, BOOM, a great voice shook the stones.

SWOOSH, the forest of legs slid backwards as if on ice.

Mup and Crow were left clear and free, gasping in the air. Slowly, Dad uncurled himself from around Tipper and Badger. Panting, they all stood up.

The crowd had been pushed into a startled semicircle, ten feet or more away. Mam stood between them and her family, her hands raised and sparking, her hair standing out in an angry cloud. "How *dare you!*" she hissed. "Stay *back.*"

There was a moment's stunned silence and then the crowd, as if on strings, dropped with a rustle and bowed their terrified faces to the stones.

Mam lowered her hands. "That's . . . that's not what I mean," she said.

But Mup thought she looked magnificent.

Across the courtyard, even the raggedy witches had fallen to their knees.

Grandmother's Castle

An astonishingly large number of dark-dressed castle people seemed very keen all of a sudden to be the ones to show Mam to the family apartments. They clustered around in jostling silence and rushed ahead on the many staircases and through the many corridors, bowing and holding out their hands to show the way. Mam marched grimly through them, Fírinne and Dad watchful at her side.

Mup trotted behind, Crow on her shoulder, Badger and Tipper at her heels. "That was amazing," she said. "*Amazing*. Did you see her?"

"Mammy zapped-ed the bad guys!" barked Tipper. "She *zoomed* them back!"

Crow muttered close to Mup's ear, his eyes fixed on Mam, who could just be glimpsed ahead of the large crowd. "That was very witchy," he muttered. "That was very, very witchy."

"Don't be afraid, Crow." Mup grinned. "Mam's on our side."

How could she ever have been worried with Mam around? How could she have forgotten for one moment what Mam had become? This was going to be easy. This was going to be great!

Mam would fix everything.

Up ahead, Mam's quiet voice could just be heard above the stiff rustle of clothes and patter of courtly feet. "We had an agreement, Fírinne. I told you I don't want anyone bowing to me."

Fírinne chuckled. "You don't understand these people," she said. "Look at them. *Gagging* to be told what to do. *Choking* for a new master. Imagine the things you could do with this power, Stella."

"People shouldn't obey me just because I'm more powerful than they are, Fírinne. They should decide for themselves how they want to live."

"Oh, would you stop! These fools couldn't decide what to have for breakfast, let alone how to rule themselves. They're too used to being told what to do."

Dad huffed. "Can't imagine anyone telling you what to do, Fírinne."

"That's why the clann were hunted almost to extinction, isn't it?" came the growled reply. "But now the whip is in our hands. Let's not—"

"I hope you're not calling me a whip," interrupted Mam softly.

"You're holding the whip," insisted Fírinne. "Don't waste the opportunity to do something useful with it. If these fools want a queen, let's give them a damned queen."

The adults faded from earshot as Mup slowed and fell behind. She looked about for the first time, taking in her remarkable surroundings. "What a confusement of staircases," she marvelled. "What a jumble of fancy rooms . . ."

On her first terrifying visit here, Mup had seen only the riverside courtyard and her grandmother's chilly throne room before being locked in the dungeons. She had supposed the entire castle would be equally as stern and terrible—but the halls she now made her way through were colourful and ornate, and the rooms that lay off them were really quite cozy.

The dungeons are still here, though. Under all this brightness. Mup looked down at her feet. Somewhere far below her—beneath all these corridors of paint and tile and polished wood—lay acres and acres of tunnels that had never seen the light of day. Mup wondered if the staff who walked these halls had ever thought of the people chained in the dark below. She wondered if they'd even known they were there.

"Where are the raggedy witches?" fretted Crow. "Are they still in the courtyard?"

Tipper bounded to a window and put his two front paws on the sill, looking out.

"Oh, we's very high up!" he barked. "Look!"

Mup and Crow crammed in at his side. They were looking down on another courtyard. The walls surrounding it were filled with graceful, diamond-paned windows, just like the one Mup now pressed her nose to. Dark archways punctured the distant base of each wall—doorways, maybe? The entrances to tunnels? There was a small green garden down there too, glowing like a flower-studded jewel.

"This is all very pretty," Mup observed. "I can't imagine the old queen liking any of it."

"Who cares what your grandma liked!" squawked Crow. "The *real* question is where have her witches gone?" Frantic now, he launched himself from Mup's shoulder and flew to the other side of the corridor. "You can see the river from this window!" he cawed.

Mup and Tipper raced across. Sure enough, this

side of the corridor looked down onto the riverside courtyard they'd just left. They were so high above everything. Mup supposed this must have been how the world had looked to her grandmother — everything small and distant, people too tiny to care about.

The great battle-scarred courtyard was empty except for one small figure. *Is that a little girl?* thought Mup. It was hard to tell. The figure was lurking in one of the dark tunnels that led to the dungeons and was so still and so grey it might have been a shadow on the wall.

Mup put her hand to the windowpane, as if to touch the small, drab figure. A sound came to her through the glass — low, distant, echoing — as though somewhere far away a dog was howling sadly in the dark. Mup was reminded again of the dungeons, of the long stretches of darkness below. She lifted her hand from the windowpane. The sound died. She put her hand back. Silence.

"Where are the witches?" repeated Crow, anxiously bobbing from foot to foot. "They were there when we came in."

"Everyone's gone," barked Tipper.

"Not everyone," murmured Mup distractedly. "There's a little girl."

"But *you* am the only girl, Mup!"

Mup shook herself and pressed forward again, straining her eyes. "But . . . I'm sure I saw a little girl."

"There are no little girls here," said a soft voice at her shoulder. "No children at all, in fact. Except for Your young Highness and her companions."

Mup spun to find a dark-clad gentleman standing very close behind her. He was very thin and very kind-looking — and it was only when he smiled that Mup realized she could see right through him.

"You're a ghost!" she exclaimed.

"A *ghost?*" cawed Crow.

"A GHOST!" barked Tipper. "A GHOST! A GHOST!"

Dad popped into view at the far end of the crowd. He stared at the ghost with some alarm.

Mup waved. *We're OK, Dad.*

Dad — a little uncertain — nodded, warily eyeing the ghost across the top of everyone's head. Following his gaze, the rest of the crowd gave the apparition just a curt glance before turning dismissively away.

The apparition sighed. "You are correct, young Highness. I am indeed a ghost. The very last one residing in the palace, to be precise — all others having followed your aunt to the other side. I do hope Your Highness shan't hold my noncorporeality against me? I can assure you that, alive or not, I am a most useful fellow."

Crow hopped up and, with a prickling of claws, perched on Mup's head. He regarded the phantom from one round eye, then the other. "You can't trust *castle people*," he said, "and you can't trust *ghosts*."

"Nonsense," said Mup. "Tipper, stop growling at the nice man."

She straightened her hat, which Crow had sent slipping over her eyes, and curtseyed. This was not an easy thing to do with a large raven balanced on her head, but it somehow felt necessary when faced with a spectral gentleman whose clothes included a ruffled lace collar and shiny buckled shoes.

Delighted, the ghost returned her bow with a flourish. "My *dear* princess, allow me to introduce myself! I am Doctor Erasmus Emberly—Doctor Emberly to my friends."

Mup opened her mouth to introduce herself, but before she could speak, Doctor Emberly neatly spun her on her heel and proceeded to herd her and Tipper and Crow ahead of him up the corridor. "Madam," he called across the crowd. "*Madam!* I have found your lost children."

"We weren't lost," objected Mup.

The staff parted before them like a retreating tide, and they found themselves right at Mam's side. The ghost could not quite hide his glee. "Madam," he beamed, bowing ornately. "Doctor Erasmus Emberly, castle physician, returning your lost children safe and sound."

"But we *weren't* lost!" insisted Mup.

"It's been a long time since there were children in the castle, madam," continued Doctor Emberly, just as if Mup hadn't spoken. "But I assure you, I am well versed in all the ailments to which infants are so often mortally prone."

"Infants?" cried Mup.

"Mortally?" cried Dad.

Mam eyed the doctor dryly. "Perhaps in the future, Doctor," she suggested, "you might wait until our children *need* your help before you inflict it on them?"

Seemingly uncertain of how best to reply, the ghost of Doctor Emberly once again bowed low. The rest of the staff—not wanting to be outdone—bowed even lower. Mam, Dad, Fírinne, Mup, Tipper, and Crow were the only people left upright in the whole crowd.

Mam pinched the bridge of her nose and took a deep breath to gather her patience. "I do *not*," she said, "want anyone *bowing*."

No one straightened.

Mup bent at the waist to be on eye level with Doctor Emberly.

"It's OK," she assured him. "Mam really means it. You don't have to bow."

As if to double-extra confirm this, Tipper licked the ghost's spectral nose.

"I know I lost my temper in the courtyard," said Mam. "I'm sorry for that. I don't want people to be frightened of me. I want everyone to feel free to speak. I want . . ."

As Mam spoke on, Mup felt an unpleasant tingling on the back of her neck. She shivered, and all around her, the staff shivered too. It was as though a breeze were gushing up everyone's spine: a shrivelling, nasty, stomach-twisting coldness entirely unlike that which comes when someone opens a window. Frowning, Mup lifted her head and looked across the crowd of bowed backs.

A small knot of raggedy witches were gliding up the corridor.

Mup straightened. Crow rose into his boy-shape. Tipper growled and Mam stopped talking.

The witches' expressionless faces glowed and faded as they passed from window-light to shade, window-light to shade. They came to a stop, gazing at Mam across the backs of the staff who continued to cower in the wave of frigid air that the witches seemed to carry with them.

"You aren't welcome here!" Mup cried. "You killed Crow's dad! You put my dad in jail!"

Still bent double, Doctor Emberly gasped. He seemed terrified that Mup would speak to the witches like that.

The witches tilted their bottomless eyes to her. One of them was much older than the others. She stepped forward, spread her cold hands, bowed her pale face, and — as if speaking for all of them — said: "We repent all previous wrongs."

"You can't just say sorry for murdering people!" cried Mup. "You can't just—"

"Mup," said Mam.

Mup spun to her in outrage.

Mam held out a hand to gently silence her. "These witches turned against the old queen, Mup. They helped us win the battle against her."

"But they're bad. They've done bad things!"

"And that will be dealt with, Mup. I promise. If people have done bad things, they'll be dealt with."

"We were only following your mother's rules," murmured the older witch. "Are we to be condemned for obeying the law, as is our duty as good citizens?"

The bowing staff glanced slyly at each other from the corners of their eyes. For the first time, Mup realized that all these stiffly dressed people with their ruffled collars and shiny shoes—all of them had spent their lives working for her grandmother. They had upheld her grandmother's laws, quietly supporting the raggedy witches from their position in the background of the queen's terrible reign.

She searched the crowd for the others who had been in the courtyard—the villagers, the river people—but they seemed to have gone. The only people who had remained after Mam's outburst were the castle staff, and they bowed now—compliant and still, as they had always been in the face of the witches' authority. Mup began to feel like there was something complicated going on, something more confusing than just beating the bad guys and rewarding the good.

Who was Mam supposed to be helping here?

"Oh, for goodness' sake," snapped Mam, startling everyone. She snagged Doctor Emberly by his transparent collar and jerked him upright. "No more bowing." She gestured to the rest of the staff. "Up!"

They straightened slowly—bewildered.

"No more bowing," said Mam. "No more fear."

29

"Majesty," warned the older witch, "a queen cannot rule without fear."

"I'm not a queen."

Something close to shock flared behind the witch leader's smooth, blank face. She glided forward. The crowd parted before her, and the other raggedy witches followed. Mup found herself looking up at them, and, with a start, she realized that, though their severe expressions and clothes made them seem ancient, the majority of these witches weren't much older than teenagers.

Is that possible? she thought. *Do raggedy witches start off as kids?* She had never thought of her grandmother's witches as anything other than grown-ups — knowing, powerful, and eternal. Another vista opened up before her now as she imagined hosts of little kids being strapped into dark uniforms, sat before pale-faced teachers, learning to be wicked, learning to be cruel.

Tipper growled nervously at her side. The witches turned their heads in unison and stared at him. Mup's heart hardened. She raised her hands. Power sparked a warning at her fingertips.

Stay away from my brother.

The lead witch was peering into Mam's face. She seemed puzzled. "If you are not a queen, what are you?"

"She's Mam," said Mup.

"And she'll *zap* you," barked Tipper.

"I'm not zapping anyone!" cried Mam. She sighed. She pinched the bridge of her nose again. "Look," she said to the witches. "I'm not here to rule."

"You defeated the old queen. It is your duty to rule."

"*We* defeated the old queen," said Mam. She indicated the people around her. She indicated Mup and Tipper and Dad. "*We* did. All of us. *Together.* And that's how things will be from now on—all of us working together. As equals."

Doctor Emberly looked up sharply at that, astonished.

"And if the old queen returns?" asked the raggedy witch.

"We'll fight her."

"We? You mean . . . ?" The witch raised a cynical eyebrow; she looked at the gaping staff.

"Yes! We! Them! *Us*. And we'll win." To the older witch's obvious consternation, Mam grabbed her shoulder. "Listen," she said. "Everyone here is born with magic. The only reason they don't use it is because my mother didn't let them learn how. You were allowed to learn—you and all the others like you. I want you to teach these people what you know. Not . . . not just *these* people, everyone. *All* the people. I want you to teach them how to use their magic."

The witch froze in horror. "You want us to give away our knowledge?"

"I want you to share it."

"Willy-nilly? With any tawdry street fool or hedge idiot? With any merchant, dress-wright, or cooper? Regardless of what they do with it? Regardless of whether or not they deserve it?"

Mam's fingers tightened on the witch's shoulder. "Everyone deserves the magic they are born with," she said. *"Everyone."*

"How will you rule, if we have no advantage over the rabble?"

"Perhaps I'm not meant to rule."

For a moment, the lead witch's face was slackened by the enormity of this suggestion. Then her expression closed over like a trap.

"You are a fool," she said.

The crowd surged aside, terrified, as the witch raised both hands. Shadows shot up the walls as her fingers blazed green fire.

Reluctantly, Mam lifted her own hands. They too were wreathed in lightning.

Mup leapt to help. Before she could so much as

shoot off a spark, a huge force slammed her and the rest of the crowd violently backwards. Mup found herself pinned against the wall, squirming uselessly. Dad and Fírinne struggled at her side. They too were pinned, as was everyone else—held against the walls, helpless to get free.

In a cleared space in the centre of the corridor, Mam and the witch stood facing each other. Mam's expression was sad, the witch's coldly angry. There was a bubble of power around them, and Mup realized that it was Mam's. Mam was keeping everyone pressed against the wall. She was keeping everyone out of harm's way.

Mup stopped struggling.

Hands still raised in warning, the raggedy witch retreated to her young followers. They gathered behind her, their eyes huge as they watched over her shoulder. "I trusted you," the witch told Mam. "You won this kingdom like a true warrior—like a queen. I thought you would be a match for your mother. Now I see you are weak."

"I am not weak," said Mam. "But I am not my mother. I will not repeat my mother's cruelties."

"I abandoned my queen for nothing."

"Not true," urged Mam. "You've given yourself the chance of life without her. You just need to be brave enough to take it." She extended a hand in invitation, allowing her lightning to die. "Share your knowledge," she said. "That's all I ask. Give others the same chances you've had."

The witch shook her head. "Never." Arms still raised to protect the young witches behind her, she began backing down the corridor.

Mam called after her. "I'm offering you a new life. You don't have to live by her rules anymore. You don't have to be so hard, and so afraid."

"You have power enough to crush us like bugs," said the witch, "but you won't. You have not the strength of character needed to rule. I was a fool to support you. You will fail. The queen will return, and she will never forgive me for betraying her. I've doomed my pupils. I've doomed myself. You've doomed us."

Mam dropped her hands. The protection magic released its grip on the crowd, and, terrified, they gathered behind her to watch the witches leave.

"You can't let them go," said Fírinne.

"I won't hold anyone here against their will."

"They're *criminals!*"

"Are they, Fírinne?" said Mam in frustration. "You told me this lot were hardly more than brainwashed schoolchildren. You told me they'd known nothing better in life and should be given a chance."

"That was when I thought they were on our side! Before you decided to let them flutter off into the sunset and do grace knows what *damage!*"

"Am I meant to arrest them just because they once worked for my mother? If that's the case, I'd have to arrest half the bloody country."

"If you don't stop them," said Dad, "they'll head straight back to her."

Mam shook her head. "I don't think they will. They're too frightened of her."

"You don't know that for sure, Stella."

"No," she sighed. "I don't — but I won't punish them for something they might do."

The raggedy witches were already far down the corridor, covering a huge distance without seeming to move at all. Mup rushed forward to keep them in sight, torn between wanting them gone and fear at what might happen if Mam allowed them to leave. Some of the staff were leaving too, creeping away in the apparent hope that no one would notice them go.

"Are you following them?" yelled Crow. "Have you forgotten what they *are?*"

"They'll protect us," whispered a retreating man. "They're strong."

Fírinne groaned. She turned to Mam again. "You need to set an example. I'm begging you. Turn those witches to stone. Set them on fire. *Anything.* Just prove that you're as strong as your mother, before everyone loses faith in you!"

Mup felt power growing in her arms and her shoulders in response to this. She felt it tingling up her spine. *Yes*, she thought, glaring at the retreating witches. *The world would be better without them. They'd deserve it. It would be easy and they'd be gone.*

Then one of the raggedy witches looked back — just a flash of pale face before she descended the stairs — and Mup understood that they were *hurrying away.* They were afraid of Mam.

You have power enough to crush us like bugs, the witch had said.

And she was right! Mam *did* have that power.

This thought filled Mup with sudden, angry glee. She clawed her sparking hands and rushed after the raggedy witches, ignoring the shouts of warning from the adults behind her. *Run!* she thought, wanting to chase the witches all the way out of the castle. *Run! I hope you've nowhere to go. I hope you have to sleep in the rain. I hope people are cruel to you and reject you and* —

She slammed to a halt at the top of the stairs, startled

by a figure below her. It was the witch who had looked back. She was all alone. The others were gone. The servants who had slunk after them were gone too. Only this one witch remained. Her eyes were jet black, her skin white as milk, just like all the raggedy witches', but she looked up at Mup with something close to terror, her body half turned away, her hand on the banister, ready to flee.

Mup stood over her in the gloom, not knowing what to think.

The witch's eyes flicked towards the sound of people running up the corridor. Then back to Mup's face. "Does she mean it?" she whispered. "Your mother. Does she mean all the things she says? Could I . . . ? Could everyone . . . ? Would your mother really allow us to use any magic? In any way we like?"

They were surrounded by tumult then: Tipper barking and barking down at the witch from the top step; Crow flying to Mup's shoulder in a fury of wings and caws; Dad pulling Mup away.

Mam and Fírinne stepped into view, and the witch shrank back.

Small and scurrying, alone possibly for the first time in her life, the witch turned to run.

Mup called to her without thinking—the words

out of her mouth before she'd even thought them. "Mam means it!" she cried. "She means everything she says . . . Stay!"

"*Stay?*" screeched Crow. "STAY? Are you *mad?*"

The witch paused for a moment, vulnerable and scared. Then — as the staff began creeping into sight behind Mam — she straightened. Her expression froze over into calm. She glided up the stairs as if she'd never felt uncertainty in her life and bowed without a trace of emotion.

Fírinne glared at her.

The staff turned from her in fear.

Mam extended her hand and said, "Welcome."

The Curse-Moon, the Silent Snow

That night, Mup lay in her bed, thinking about the witch, and how scared the castle staff had been of her, and how Mam had allowed her to stay. She thought about how angry that had made Fírinne. "Her kind has just proved they can't be trusted," she'd hissed. "They've proved they can't change. You can't let her join us after that. You can't treat her like she is one of us!"

Eventually, Mam had had to have the witch locked in a guarded room. The witch had remained calm and poised and expressionless through it all. She'd said nothing when they'd closed and locked the door to her little prison.

I wonder what she's doing now? thought Mup. *Has she gone to bed like a normal person? Is she hanging from the ceiling like a bat?*

Mup wasn't afraid—not even a little bit. She lifted her arms from under the duvet and held her hands out in front of her face. Sparks danced lazily from fingertip to fingertip. *I'm like Mam*, she thought. *No one can hurt me. No one will ever hurt my friends.*

If they tried, she'd blast them.

She waggled her glowing fingers. They left trails of light in the dark. Delighted, Mup drew a smiley face in the air, and as the face faded, she drew a heart. She popped a daisy in the middle. Mup laughed, then looked guiltily across at the door that separated her bedroom from Crow's. She let her arms drop back onto the duvet, and the light-pictures dispersed in a shower of glitter.

Crow wasn't happy right now. He especially wasn't happy with Mup.

She'd tried to talk to him about it, but he'd blanked her. When Dad had shown him his new room, Crow had just walked inside and shut the door on all their faces, and that had been that.

"Leave him be awhile," Dad had said, gently turning Mup and Tipper from the door. "None of this can be easy for him."

"It's 'cos Mup is fwiends with the raggedy witch!" barked Tipper.

I never said I was her friend, thought Mup. *I just felt sorry for her. Anyway, she's not a raggedy witch. Not anymore . . . She chose Mam. That means she's a good guy now. Right?*

Mup shivered suddenly. Her arms were chilly. She snuggled back down under the duvet, pulling the covers to her chin. Surely it hadn't been this cold a minute ago?

Her new bedroom was a cavernous space around her, her bed tiny within it, her wardrobe and bookshelves miles away across acres of stone floor. The little fire that Mam had lit in the big fireplace cast a warm glow around the room—but something was changing. Mup felt it in the air. Something was wrong.

She frowned, listening.

What was that sound at her window? Mup could just about hear it above the crackle of the fire: soft, almost sly, a barely audible *pat, pat, pat* against the glass.

Still under the covers, Mup pulled on her polka-dot dressing gown and fluffy pink socks. She slipped out into the frigid air, crept to the window, and opened her curtains.

Her room filled with harsh white light, and Mup stared up into the big hard face of a full moon. It must have risen while she was in bed. Now it floated above the castle, bloated and bullyish, its light dominating the sky.

41

A witch moon, thought Mup. *That's not good.*

The last time the moon had been like this, Aunty Boo had died.

The last time it had been like this, raggedy witches had come to steal Mam.

Through the cruel moonlight, snow was falling. Not the usual fluttering gentleness but an endless, busy, determined weight—as if this snow were working hard at something, as if it were trying to erase the world. When Mup had gone to bed, there hadn't been a cloud in the sky. Now the roofs were muffled white. The riverside courtyard that lay beneath her window was smothered, the rubble hidden, the battle scars obliterated.

Mup pulled her dressing gown tight. *It's just snow*, she told herself. *You like snow.* But even as she thought this, she backed away from the knowing gaze of the moon, into the shadows that poured restlessly down the walls of her room. It reminded her of her grandmother, that moon—the cold, hard way it stared at her, the way it blotted out the fragile stars.

She faltered, wondering if she should get Mam or Dad. They were in the library, just across the little sitting room that all their new bedrooms opened onto. If Mup opened her door and called they'd come running. But

Mam and Dad were in a meeting with Fírinne and some people who had arrived late in the evening. They were the ones who had fled after Mam's outburst—the ones who weren't castle people. They had crept back warily, bowing and scared but hoping to talk. Mam had *begged* Mup not to interrupt. Breaking in now with some complaint about the snow was probably a terrible idea.

Mup crept to the small wooden door that joined her bedroom to Crow's.

Tentatively, she knocked.

"Crow?" she whispered. She pushed open the door. Crow's room was slashed with moonlight. It sliced through his open curtains, casting uneasy shadows on his bedroom walls.

"Crow? Have you seen the—?"

Mup came up short. Crow's bed was empty. The covers unslept in. She looked around the bare space. Mam and Dad had brought the bed from their spare room at home. There was no other furniture. No Crow either—not standing in the shadows or perched on the curtain rails or huddled by the crackling fire.

A window was open. Reluctantly, Mup edged into watchful moonlight and peeped outside. Bird footprints tacked away across the snow-muffled sill. There was a small flurry at the edge where Crow must have launched himself into the air. Mup opened the window wide and leaned out, looking up to the moon-washed battlements for her friend. Her whisper came out on a silver puff of breath.

"Crow?"

No reply.

Mup paused, aware of the extreme silence. All around her, flake after flake of snow added its weight to the breathless quiet, and despite the constant downward movement, the stillness felt complete. She leaned further out of the window.

There was a person in the courtyard below.

"Crow!" she whispered. "You'll catch your death."

But the shadowy figure was not Crow — not unless he'd taken to wearing a dress, not unless his hair had got very flat and long. Mup realized, with a start, that it was the little girl again — the one she'd glimpsed before the ghost of Doctor Emberly had startled her and the raggedy witches had driven everything else from her mind.

The girl was in the exact spot Mup had seen her before: loitering in one of the tunnels that led up from the dungeons. She was like a mouse in its hole, all afraid of a cat. She cowered. She cringed. Her eyes darted here and there. After a while, she seemed to find enough courage to creep to the mouth of the tunnel and, as though wondering at the snow, peered out.

Poor thing, thought Mup. *She's so afraid.*

"She shouldn't be here," croaked a hoarse voice from the lintel above Mup's head.

She twisted to find Crow glowering down at her. He fluttered to the windowsill and glared into the courtyard. "Your mother should chase her away."

"Chase her away? But she's just a little girl."

He snapped his bright gaze to her. "Just a *little girl?*"

"Well . . . yes," said Mup. "I feel sorry for her, all alone in the cold like that."

This seemed to outrage Crow. "She *should* be in the cold. She *deserves* to be in the cold. Do you think she was *made* to become a witch? Well, she wasn't. They *chose* to serve the queen. They *chose* to do any terrible thing she asked them. And now she thinks she can swan around like she's never done anything wrong? Live in the castle? Move into *our* family and—"

"Crow, what are you talking about? Calm down!"

But Crow was so angry Mup thought his feathers might pop out. "Calm *down*? Am I the only one with any sense? While you've been in bed, asleep like a castle-born fool, *I've* been watching her. She's been wandering around for hours, staring up at the curse-moon with that . . . that witchy look on her pasty face. Don't you tell me she's not up to something!"

"Wandering around . . . ?"

Astounded, Mup looked back down. She ducked at the sight of a dark figure standing in the courtyard below. It was the witch! The one who was meant to be locked up! She was nothing but a glimmer of pale skin in the shadows of the broken wall. She stood motionless, gazing up into the broad plate of the moon.

Mup realized that she'd been so intrigued by the little girl that she hadn't seen a raggedy witch standing right under her window — and Crow had been so upset by the witch that he hadn't noticed the little girl, cold and alone in the snow.

"What's she doing?" Mup whispered.

"*Precisely!*" hissed Crow. "What *is* she doing?"

The witch was doing exactly what Crow had described, standing in the snow, looking up at the moon. Her pale hands were clasped against her breast, her pale face upturned to the light. Her expression was completely blank — yet somehow anxious.

In the tunnel on the other side of the courtyard, the little girl had also noticed the witch. She froze at first, terrified. Then her pinched little face contracted in anger. Her brows drew down in hate.

Her mouth pulled itself into a bitter shape.

The little girl drifted back into the shadows. Still staring at the witch, she turned sideways against the wall. She pressed sideways against the wall. There was a strange, subtle pucker—like a stone dropping into dark water—and then she was gone.

The little girl had passed right through the wall of the castle.

"My goodness," whispered Mup. "She's a ghost."

"What are you bleating about?" cried Crow, his attention still on the witch. "She's as solid as you and me! Look at her! She—" He startled. He stilled. He drew in closer to Mup. "She's seen us," he whispered.

Sure enough, down in the courtyard, the raggedy witch was looking up at them.

And then the witch was coming towards them. Floating upwards as the heavy snow fell down, she rose lightly through the moonlight. Up and up she came until she was right outside Crow's window, her dark, oval eyes level with Mup's, her toes neatly pointed at the distant ground. She was cool and graceful and elegant. Effortless and calm.

"Let me in," she said.

Crow—not at all elegant or calm—exploded. "This is my room!" he cried. "No witches allowed!"

"I must speak with the queen," said the witch.

"Why do you need Mam?" asked Mup.

The witch lifted her polished face to the falling snow. "Can you not feel it? This snow. That moon. They are not natural. Your mother must be warned."

"Take the stairs, then!" cawed Crow. "Fly down a chimney! You can't just waft up here and climb into my room! You're meant to be *locked up*. You're meant to be *in jail*. Why—?"

"Hush, Crow," said Mup.

"*Hush?*" he sputtered.

"Yes. Hush." Mup turned once again to the witch. Her eyes were dark and unfathomable. Her hair and clothes drifted gently against the backdrop of falling snow. She seemed willing to wait in silence, just bobbing outside Crow's window, as if knowing it was only a matter of time before Mup let her in.

"What . . . what is your name?" asked Mup.

"What does her *name* have to do with it?"

"Oh, *hush*, Crow! It just feels important." And it did feel important. As if by telling Mup her name, the witch would be paying the highest price possible to access Crow's room.

The witch drifted lightly backwards, seeming troubled. "I do not have a name."

"Of course you do." Mup frowned. "Everyone has a name. What did your mam and dad call you?"

"My parents' name for me does not count."

"I don't understand."

Crow huffed. "She gave up her name when she joined the queen's witches — her *name*, her *family*. Everything. They all do."

The floating witch simply turned her black eyes to him and said nothing.

He shook his glossy head. "All so you could do some *magic*."

"I am good at magic," said the witch softly.

"If you were *that* good, the queen would have given you a new name. You'd have been proud enough to tell us *that* one, wouldn't you?"

The witch dropped her eyes. "I was never very good at the queen's magic," she said.

Crow ruffled his feathers, satisfied. "Well, it's too late now. The queen is gone and you're left with nothing. No name. No family. Nothing. You should have chosen a better life."

"Maybe she's trying to do that now, Crow," suggested Mup gently.

"Not by climbing in my window, she's not."

"But she needs to get to Mam."

"This is my room. Your mam said so!"

"But just this once, Crow."

"How can it be MY ROOM if you get to decide what HAPPENS IN IT?"

"Naomi," said the witch.

They both turned to her in exasperation. "What?" they snapped.

"Naomi. The name my mother gave me."

"Oh," said Crow.

"Naomi," said Mup.

The witch winced, just slightly.

Mup repeated the name again. "Naomi . . . I like it. It suits you."

The witch bobbed gently in the air, snow falling all around her. Her expression was as impassive as ever, but Mup thought that she had changed somehow. She couldn't explain it. The witch just seemed more real—truer—now that Mup knew her name. Her face was less of a mask.

Mup pushed Crow's window further open and stepped back. "Come in," she said.

"No . . ." gasped Crow as the witch floated past him and stepped down into his room.

Her cloak swept his windowsill, brushing snow onto his rug.

She tracked wet footprints onto his floor.

Mup ran ahead and opened the door. "Aren't you coming, Crow?"

The witch stepped between them, blocking Mup's view. "We cannot afford delay."

Mup leaned around her. "Crow?"

"This was meant to be my room," he whispered. "Your mam said so."

"It's just this once, Crow. I promise. No raggedy witches after tonight."

Crow just continued to stare at her from the windowsill, his round eyes glittering in the moonlight. After a moment, Mup turned reluctantly from him and led the witch across the sitting room. At the library, she stopped with her hand on the doorknob.

"Naomi," she said. "Try not to scare everyone when you go inside, OK?"

But the witch was not behind her. She had paused halfway across the room and was standing in front of the sitting-room fire. Tipper was asleep there in his dog basket, Badger curled around him. The witch was staring at them, her head tilted to one side. As Mup watched, she crouched down and reached to touch Tipper's peaceful face. Her expression was one of almost yearning. She looked very young.

"Are you still in school, Naomi? Fírinne said you and your friends were schoolchildren."

The witch's fingers closed in on themselves. Her yearning expression disappeared, as if sucked under ice. "I have studied here for ten years."

"Here? There's a school in the castle? My mam's planning to start a school here—for kids to learn magic. I didn't know there was one here already."

"My parents placed me under the queen's tutelage when I was eight. It was for my own good. I needed protection from my failings." The witch stood up and folded her hands. Her silence and composure were so complete that Mup wasn't sure what to say for a moment. It was hard to believe that Naomi was only eighteen. She looked far too still—far too cold—to be a teenager.

"That . . . that woman with you today, was she your teacher? She seemed mean."

"Our tutor is good to us," said the witch. "She teaches us right from wrong." She gestured to Tipper. "Will no one do the same for this wayward child? Does no one love him enough to protect him from the consequences of his aberration?"

Mup felt her expression harden. She didn't know the meaning of the word "aberration," but she was not at all happy with the suggestion that Tipper—fast asleep in all his innocence—was doing something wrong.

"You mean, because he's a puppy? Tipper can be whatever he wants, Naomi."

"That is outlawed."

"Not anymore, it's not."

The witch flinched at that, a tiny moment of uncertainty—or maybe of disapproval.

Mup said coldly, "I thought you wanted to talk to my mam?"

The witch glided forward, and Mup opened the library door.

At the sight of the raggedy witch looming in the doorway, the occupants of the library leapt to their feet in a clatter of toppled chairs. These were no castle folk, only plain-dressed river people, round-faced villagers: a gathering of ordinary citizens. They stampeded in fear to the other side of the room. Only Mam and Dad and Fírinne moved against the tide of panic.

"Get away from my child!" yelled Dad, storming forward to pull Mup from Naomi's side.

Doctor Emberly seethed luminously at his shoulder. His hitherto gentle face was coldly angry. "And you wonder why so few people had the courage to return to this meeting," he snapped to Mam. "What do you expect, after you allow one of them free roam of the castle?"

"What are you doing here?" cried Fírinne to the witch. "Where are your guards?"

Naomi held up a hand to stop her. There was no fire at the witch's fingertips, no hint of lightning, but Fírinne came to a halt nonetheless, eyeing the upraised hand with bitter frustration. "You best not have hurt the men and women I left guarding you."

"They sleep," said Naomi. "That is all."

Mam, calm amid the fury and fear, said, "You agreed to stay where I put you until you were called. Was I a fool to trust you?"

"Something is wrong," said the witch. "I came to tell you."

"I let her in through the bedroom window, Mam," said Mup.

"You came through our child's *window*?" cried Dad.

"It was the quickest route," said Naomi.

"Through her *window*?"

"The moon is wrong," said Naomi. "The snow too."

"The *moon*?" Dad sputtered. "The *snow*?"

But the natives of Witches Borough rushed to the windows as if knowing precisely what Naomi meant. They pulled the heavy curtains aside. A cold, terrified stillness came over them as they gazed out at the bloated moon.

"A curse-moon," whispered Fírinne. "The old queen is watching us."

People stood aside as Mam came and leaned on the sill. She stared calmly up into the sky. Her dark eyes seemed to hold the moon's light within them — twin highlights in liquid black. "Hello, Mother," she whispered.

"She has cursed you," said Naomi. "She has cursed this place."

"I knew your mother wasn't truly gone," snarled Fírinne to Mam. "We should have hunted her and her minions down after the battle. Burned them all."

"If I recall correctly," said Dad dryly, eyeing the people cowering on the far side of the room, "you were a little short on volunteers."

"Do you think it's too late to leave?" whispered one of the visitors.

"The old queen knows we're here," whispered another. "The moon will have told her."

"Shhh," Doctor Emberly urged them. "Don't say another word. She'll hear you."

The people pressed their hands to their mouths. They edged to the corners of the room, as if being near to each other somehow made things worse.

Emberly drifted to look out of the window. "That snow is very bad. Oh, you poor creatures. She'll smother you with it. She'll freeze you. You must leave before she buries you."

"But it's just *snow*," cried Mup. "It's just a *moon*! We still have our voices, don't we? The moon can't stop us speaking! We still have arms and legs and feet. No amount of snow could bury us—not when we can work together to dig ourselves out!"

"You don't understand," mourned Emberly. "You don't understand. These poor people . . ."

Mam looked hard at the distraught ghost, then at the others, who were all staring at the window, doomed expressions on their faces. "No," she said. "I suppose we don't." She gently drew the curtains shut and resumed her seat at the table. Mup thought she looked very strong and upright sitting on her own, her hands folded on the polished wood.

"I don't know how curses work," Mam said. "How do we beat this?"

The room stayed silent, everyone staring at the curtains.

"Why won't you *answer* her?" cried Mup.

Fírinne took a seat by Mam, suddenly heavy and defeated, all her fire gone. "They won't answer because there's nothing to say. A curse is a curse. It can't be beat."

Mam took Fírinne's hand.

The gesture seemed to startle Fírinne, then to comfort her. "I thought we'd won, Stella."

"But we did!" cried Mup.

Dad squeezed her shoulders. "Of course we did." But looking up at him, standing so tall above her, Mup could see the uncertainty in his broad face.

"So the old queen uses curses now," murmured Doctor Emberly's ghost.

Fírinne huffed. "Where have you been for the last half-century? The old queen has been cursing people for as long as I can remember."

"My dear lady, the queen executed me over seventy-five years ago. I've been trapped in her dungeons ever since . . . I freely admit to being hopelessly out of touch."

"Oh," said Fírinne. "Sorry. You look so young."

"How kind!" Doctor Emberly grinned. "One does try." He adjusted his jacket, momentarily bumped from his despondency, then quickly lost his sparkle. "You know," he said, "when I died, most people thought the queen was simply going through a phase. No one seriously believed she would take *everyone's* magic. They thought she was just clearing out a few inconvenient eccentrics. A few outrageous freethinkers . . . Like me." He glanced at Naomi, who still stood like a pillar of ice in the doorway. "No one ever believes the witches will

57

come for them. Until, of course, they wake up to find one of them standing at the foot of their bed."

Everyone looked at the raggedy witch. She stared impassively back.

"I don't know any more about the queen's curses than the rest of you," she said. "I had only begun to learn from her. I had not yet even earned a name."

"Your name is Naomi," Mup reminded her. "And you know more about the queen than anyone else here."

The witch grimaced.

Fírinne growled.

Mam sighed. "It seems like you're all we've got, Naomi."

"She is *not* all you've got," snapped Fírinne. "What about *us*? The ones who stood *beside* you and *fought* for you? The ones who spent their lives suffering under the likes of *her*. Have you any idea how hard it is to listen to you make up to these creatures after all they've done to us?"

Emberly turned from his mournful contemplation of the snow. His expression was bitter now, his voice like quiet acid. "Oh, but they are *useful*, aren't they? The new queen *needs* them. Of course she does—because they are the only ones left with any *knowledge*. They are the only ones left with any *experience*. They've spent

58

decades murdering the best among us—all the time convincing the rest of us that we couldn't, *shouldn't* think for ourselves. And now they are the only ones left who know *anything!*"

Mam surprised him by taking his hand. "You're still here, Doctor," she said. "Thank you for choosing to stay. I'm grateful for your knowledge and your memories."

"I . . . I only ever wanted to be useful, madam."

"You *are* useful."

Mam turned to Fírinne. "My brave friend," she said, "rest assured that *nothing* is forgotten."

Emberly's and Fírinne's faces softened in gratitude. But they hardened again just as quickly when Mam turned to the raggedy witch. "I need your help." She raised a hand to silence Fírinne's renewed outrage. "I need your help," she repeated to the witch. "Come in."

Naomi glided expressionlessly into the room.

Mam turned her attention to Mup. "Do you need someone to accompany you back to your room, Mup?"

"Amn't I staying?" cried Mup.

Dad turned her sharply on her heel and pushed her out of the door. "No," he said. "You are not."

"But . . ."

Dad leaned down to face her. "I don't have to tell you not to open your window for any more witches, do I?"

"But, Dad!"

"Because I wouldn't be pleased," he said. "I wouldn't be pleased *at all* to find out you'd do something like that twice."

He stared firmly into her eyes until she relented.

"I won't, Dad."

"Good. Because it's not just you you're risking, you know. It's Tipper and Crow too. They're not like you, Mup. They don't have the same . . ." Dad wiggled his fingers, as if conjuring lightning. "You need to remember that."

Mup humphed. Dad didn't have to worry about Tipper and Crow; Mup had enough lightning to protect them all. "What about the curse?" she demanded. "What about the snow?"

"Leave that to your mother," said Dad, and he gently shut the door.

The sitting room closed its quiet around her. Tipper was snoring in his dog basket. He was so peaceful and happy. A little tingle of chill ran up Mup's spine when she remembered the expression on Naomi's face as she'd stood over him.

Badger's eyes opened sleepily in the firelight.

"It's OK, Badger," whispered Mup. "Go back to sleep. I won't let anyone hurt him."

Badger softly thumped his tail and closed his eyes.

"And I won't let my grandma hurt anyone either," she said. "Crow!" She ran to her friend's room. "Crow! Naomi says there's a curse. How do we—?"

She halted on the threshold. Crow's window was still open. Cold was pouring in, and snow had piled high, gleaming and somehow gleeful in the emptiness of the room. Naomi's footprints were frozen to ice on the floor.

"Crow?" Mup went to the window. "Crow, where are you?"

Only silence answered her. She looked down to the tunnel where the grey figure of the little girl had been. It was empty, but the shadows there felt watchful and populated, judging her.

Mup was angry suddenly. Angry that she'd so much to tell and no one to tell it to. Angry that her friend wasn't around when she needed him to explain things.

Oh, why did Crow always have to be so difficult! Why did he have to make things so hard?

What difference did it make to let Naomi into his room?

She slammed her hand on the windowsill, little sparks of frustration shooting from her fingertips.

"I know you're there, you stubborn bird! I know you can hear me! Crow? Crow! It was just *one time*! There are more important things going on than a witch coming through your window!"

But there was no sign or sound of her friend, just the relentless snow tumbling down, the judgmental shadows by the wall, and the moon gloating in the watchful sky.

The Drawing in the Hall

Hi Mup,
Mam has to go say goodbye to last night's
visitors. Firinne and I are going with her.
We'll only be down in the riverside courtyard.
Look out of your window and you'll see us. We
didn't want to wake you. Crow already seems
to be up and about. (I think we need to have
a word with him about leaving his window
open!) The ghost of Doctor Emberly said he'd
keep an eye on Tipper and Badger (you don't
need looking after, of course!). He is in the
library if you need anything. Will be back
before you know it and we'll go exploring.
   Love,
   Dad

The note—written in Dad's square, cheerful hand—had been on Mup's pillow when she woke up. She read it sitting up in bed, then sat looking at the door that led to Crow's room. It was open. She could see inside. His window was firmly shut, and someone had mopped his floor. His bed looked unslept in.

Mup had not meant to fall asleep. She'd only climbed into bed to get warm, and she'd lain there watching through Crow's door, waiting for him to return. At first, she had fumed over him leaving. Then she had fretted over him being out in the snow. And then, at some stage, in her warm, cozy bed, she must have dropped off.

Outside, snow still fell and fell and fell.

Mup wondered if her stubborn friend had spent the whole night out in it.

Please be OK, Crow.

She leaned out of bed and reached down to the floor, thinking to press her hand to the ground and find Crow that way. Then she hesitated, half in, half out of bed, her hand hovering. Would it be right to do that? If Crow wanted to be on his own, would it be right for Mup to find him—just because she could—and force him to come back inside?

It's for his own good, she thought, frowning. *He's being* silly staying out in the cold and wasting the lovely bed Mam and Dad gave him. Still . . . Mup's fingers curled in on themselves. Still . . . Was it right for her to use magic to make Crow do something he might not want to do?

Voices came drifting up from the yard, and, still frowning, Mup crept from bed to see what was going on. Far below, a small group of people came into view. It was Mam's visitors from the library. Mam was with them, striding along in her padded winter coat and boots, her hands thrust deep in her pockets. She was speaking quietly and insistently.

"I will not force anyone to work with me," she said. "But you understand, don't you, nothing will improve if we don't stand against my mother's ways. If you want change, you must speak for change. Otherwise, everyone will shrink back into silence, thinking they're alone."

The people with her kept nodding and nodding, but Mup didn't think they were truly listening. They kept staring up into the sky, as though afraid it was watching them. Huddled against the constantly falling snow, they seemed in a great hurry to leave.

Dad and Fírinne followed behind, stalking through the snow with matching strides, their heads swivelling left and right. There were no ravens on the broken walls today, and no cats patrolling the shadows. *Who's on guard?*

thought Mup. *Surely not just Fírinne and Dad?*

She pressed closer to the windowpane, craning to see everything at once.

At the top of the boat steps, the visitors paused, seeming uncertain how to say goodbye. Mam stuck out her hand. Instead of shaking it, the others looked sideways at each other and then bowed. Mam sighed. Her hand returned to her pocket. She nodded, and the visitors left at once—jostling to be the first down the boat steps and onto the waiting raft.

Already their footprints were disappearing under the snow.

Soon it would be as if they'd never been here at all.

Mam was left at the top of the steps, snow gathering on her head and shoulders, watching the raft float away into the mist. Mup did not like how sad and disappointed she seemed—how sad and disappointed these people had made her. Mam was just trying to help, and they wouldn't even listen to her. They were running away because of the *weather*. Because someone had told them they were *cursed*.

"I wouldn't believe I was cursed until someone proved it to me," muttered Mup. "You wouldn't catch *me* running away because of some snow." Oh, why was Mam even bothering? "These people are too timid. Mam should just *make* them cooperate."

There was a bright flash and Mup recoiled, startled to find her fingers dancing with fire. That distant howl echoed in her head again — the long, desperate mourning of a dog left alone in the dark. Smoke curled from the windowsill and Mup stared at the smouldering handprints her anger had scorched into the wood.

"Daddy!" barked Tipper, his words ringing bright and clear in the yard below. "Daddy! Look at me! Weeeeeee!" His voice was a sunny, almost painful contrast to the sorrowful howl that still ghosted through Mup's mind. Hands clenched, she watched as her brother barrelled into sight and dived into the pristine snow, a fat-pawed, yellow-furred streak of happiness bursting through the tension.

"Look how far I can goes!" he barked.

Tipper slid across the yard on his belly, showering snow and leaving a wide path in his wake. Dad and Fírinne skipped aside as he passed between them like a snowplough. They were both avalanched. Fírinne sputtered. Dad laughed. He dived for Tipper. "I thought Doctor Emberly was looking after you, you little divil!"

Mup found herself frowning as father and son tumbled away in a flurry of white.

How could they be so silly?

"You're a *naughty* puppy." Dad laughed, rolling

Tipper onto his back and tickling his tummy. "Naughty, naughty boy, running away from the poor doctor!"

Mam was distractedly watching the visitors sail away. "I wish I could understand why this so-called curse frightens them. It's just snow."

"It is not just *snow*," said Fírinne, darkly. She tightened her arms against her chest and glowered out into the wall of mist that now hid the retreating boat. "You wait and see. Something terrible will happen soon."

Dad, Tipper cradled in his arms, regarded the two women solemnly for a moment. Then a mischievous look came over his face. He slyly gathered a handful of snow. "Well," he said, "curse or no curse, it'd be a shame to waste such a glorious downfall."

And he flung a snowball, hitting Mam right in the back of the head.

Fírinne gasped. Tipper laughed. Far above them all, Mup frowned and frowned.

How could Dad be such a clown when there was so much important stuff happening?

Down in the yard, Mam stood expressionlessly, snow pattering from her hair onto the shoulders of her coat. "You threw a snowball at me," she said.

Dad's hand curled in on itself. He seemed all a-tingle with glee.

"The kingdom is crumbling around us," said Mam, "and you threw a *snowball* at me."

To Mup's immense surprise, Mam stooped, scooped a double handful, and straightened. "Prepare to die," she told Dad.

Tipper howled in happiness, Dad grinned, and, to Fírinne's obvious astonishment, the air around her filled with shrieks and delighted barks and showers of loose-flung snow.

Mup blinked. She watched Mam and Dad running about flinging snow at each other, and her hands slowly unclenched. Why was she so angry? They were just being happy, that was all. They were happy. That wasn't a crime.

She pressed her fingers to the angry burn marks on the windowsill.

She listened, waiting to hear if the dog would howl again. The dog remained silent.

Those poor people in the raft, thought Mup. *They have every right to be scared. We don't know half of what the old queen put them through.* Mam was right. It was no use pushing people around and making them do what she wanted—even if it was best for them in the end. *We'd be no better than Grandma then.* They had to find a way that didn't involve scaring people half to death.

In the meantime?

Mup smiled down at her happy family. In the meantime, there were snowballs to be thrown.

Leaning out into the frosty air, Mup yelled, "Wait for me!"

She went to shut the window, but a movement on the far side of the yard caught her eye and she paused. Her heart leapt when she saw a small figure moving through the darkness of the opposite tunnel — slowly, slowly creeping forward, as if reluctantly drawn by the sound of laughter.

The grey girl stopped at the edge of the shadows, hugging the wall. Her bright, mouselike eyes followed Mup's family as they ran chaotically about. Mup watched a series of expressions cross the girl's ashy features. At first, there was just fear — the girl winced at every shriek, shrank back at every upflung shower of snow. Then confusion took fear's place. Then a more complex expression settled on the girl's face.

Mup recognized this final expression. She had felt a version of it herself only moments ago, when Dad — despite all the terrible things going on in the world — had had the audacity to throw a snowball and have some fun. It was as though the little grey girl had looked at Mup's family — laughing and dancing and messing about in the snow — and decided they were wicked. She saw them happy, and she condemned them for it. She saw them happy, and she wanted them punished.

Mup did not know why this sent such a spear of alarm through her. After all, the girl was so small and so shy, what harm could she possibly do? But Mup felt a sudden strong need to protect her family. She felt a need to protect them from the little grey girl.

Urgently, she leaned out of the window, scanning the parapets for Crow. There was no sign of him, so Mup threw back her head and cawed as loudly as she could. It was the special call Crow had taught her, their *I'm in trouble* call. If Crow heard it — even if he was still angry with her — Mup knew he'd come quick.

Just before she slammed the window shut, she glanced back down into the courtyard. The grey girl still scowled from the shadows.

Stay right there, Mup thought.

Still in her dressing gown and pyjamas, Mup flung open her bedroom door. Across the sitting room, the library door was open. She could see Badger in there, fast asleep by the fire. Doctor Emberly was also in the library, poring shortsightedly through a book. The ghost was holding the pages very close to his face, turning each one with a wave of his transparent finger. He'd become so absorbed that he didn't seem to realize he was floating ten feet in the air.

Some babysitter you are, Mup thought, dashing across the sitting room in her stockinged feet. *I bet I could cartwheel across this room and you wouldn't see me.*

Sure enough, Doctor Emberly did not even hear her opening the hall door; he simply kept on studying, his luminous face intent, his lips moving gently as he read.

How different he was to the dark and creeping grey girl.

Mup shut the door on the turning of pages and the cozy crackle of the fire. The corridor was endless, lined with tall and gloomy windows, and she was immediately filled with impatience. Oh, why was this castle so ridiculously big? Why were there so many hallways and stairs and passages?

She took off running as fast as she could.

Her fluffy socks had no grip at all on the slippery marble floor. She could barely keep her feet. *I'll take forever to get to the courtyard!* she thought. *If I was Crow, I'd just fly out of the window! If I was Naomi, I'd float. Even Doctor Emberly can levitate. And here I am, slithering about like an idiot.*

Oh no, here came a corner! And . . . oh no, Mup couldn't stop!

She skidded in a long, desperate arc. Her feet went in every direction.

Her legs went out behind her, and she fell.

Mup's face slammed towards the floor. But she never hit the ground.

Instead, there was the strangest flipping sensation. Mup's feet swept up over her head; her hair brushed the floor as she spun a dizzying cartwheel. For a moment, her head was swaddled in a tangle of pink-and-yellow polka-dot dressing gown. Then she righted herself, her dressing gown fell back into place, and Mup realized that she was bobbing about in midair.

Whoa! she thought, flinging her arms out for balance. *Whoa!*

She wobbled, thrown by the sensation of nothing beneath her feet.

And then she thought, almost fiercely, *Why not? Why NOT me?* After all, so many astonishing things had already happened, finding she could fly was hardly the strangest.

Mup knitted her brow, jutted her chin, and leaned forward.

Faster! she thought and, just like that, she put on speed.

Toes neatly pointed, arms straight by her sides, Mup shot through the pearly strips of light thrown by snow-patted windows. The breeze pushed back her cloud of dark hair.

This was amazing! This was great!

But what would Crow think?

He'd think I look like a raggedy witch.

Mup lost her smile. She slammed to a halt at the head of a set of stairs.

A stairwell dropped away below her, and she hovered over it, her toes inches from the top step. *I don't have to fly any further,* she thought. *I can always just run the rest of the way.*

But why *should* she run? Why shouldn't she fly, if she could? It was part of her — this talent — it was part of who she was. Why would anyone want to stop her from being who she was?

Mup floated a little further out, her fingers brushing the banisters. Her toes were half a foot above the top of the second step. All she had to do was slide down the air: down and down, round and round, flight after flight, without ever touching a step, all the way to the bottom. It would be very easy — much easier than running. Besides, the little grey girl was down there watching Mup's family with that look on her face — as if playing in the snow was the worst crime anyone could ever commit.

I'm doing it, thought Mup, and she dropped into the dark.

The light from a landing window flashed and was gone.

Around a corner she zipped, and down the chequered tiles of a black-and-white corridor. Snow tapped softly against a rapid succession of stained-glass windows. Mup didn't hesitate at the top of the next stairs—she just shot downwards. The steps ticked by like counters.

Whoosh, past windowless wooden panels. *Zip*, down a spiral staircase.

Mup's hair streamed back from her forehead, her eyes widened with delight.

This was wonderful. It was *wonderful*. She quite forgot Crow's disapproval. She quite forgot her desire to catch the little grey girl. Everything was lost in the sheer rush of flying.

The second-floor corridor sped past, its yellow stone columns a blur.

Over the top of the last flight of stairs, and down, down, down, and round the corner of the ground-floor corridor, and there was Crow, standing in the middle of the hall.

Mup dropped from the air, stumbled the last few steps, and knocked into him. He was — for once — in his boy-shape, and thankfully he was staring in the opposite direction.

He had not seen her fly.

"Crow!" she cried, too brightly, straightening them both from where she'd flung them into the wall. "How are you?" Her hands came away all dirty. Her friend was covered in soot. "Crow, have you been up a chimney?"

Crow just grabbed her by the arm and urgently pulled her into the shadows.

"Shh," he said. "Don't make a sound,
Something odd is going down."

Uh-oh, thought Mup. He's rhyming.

"What is it?" she whispered. "Is it the ghost girl? I saw her too. I—"

Crow impatiently shushed her again. He pointed silently to the corridor ahead. There was a butler there, kneeling on the floor by the wall.

"I don't trust castle people," said Crow.
"But this chap seems a bit upset,
Do you think he needs a . . . a . . . pet?"

Indeed, tears were positively pouring down the butler's face. He sobbed brokenheartedly, and as he wept, he scrubbed and scrubbed at a drawing that had

76

been scrawled on the wall. Squinting, Mup could just about make out a mangled-looking bird. Or was it a fish? The drawing was no longer very clear.

"I'm so sorry," sobbed the butler, pausing to dab his wet cheeks with his duster. "I'm so, so sorry. I wish I'd done something . . ."

Seemingly overcome, he leaned against the wall, and the duster—now quite soggy with his tears—cleaned the last of the drawing from the wood.

Abruptly confused, the butler sat back.

Mup risked approaching him. "Are you OK?" she asked. "Would you like a hanky?"

Realizing she didn't actually have a hanky, Mup offered the sleeve of her polka-dot dressing gown. It seemed a perfectly reasonable alternative, but the butler just blinked at it.

"I . . . I was sent to clean a drawing from the lower hall wainscotting," he said.

"Bit much for you, was it?" asked Crow. "Bit of a strain on the nerves?"

The butler seemed to notice that he was on his knees, slumped like limp lettuce against the wall, a soggy duster in his hand. "Well," he blustered, springing to his feet and straightening his ruffled collar. "Well." He tucked the duster into his back pocket. "With all due respect to the new queen, we're not used to children scrawling on the walls. Perhaps the young princess might consider confining her artistic endeavours to the paper provided for her schooling."

"I didn't draw on the wall," said Mup.

But the butler was already retreating up the corridor, the duster making a damp patch on the rear of his trousers.

"What a strange man," she said.

"They're all strange here," muttered Crow. "Sobbing his heart out because you drew on his wall."

"It wasn't *me*," insisted Mup.

"Well, certainly Crow is not the culprit!

Maybe little brother did it."

Mup raised a dubious eyebrow. These days, Tipper was more interested in barking and running around on four paws than anything else.

"I can't think who else it would be," said Crow reluctantly, as if loath to get Tipper into trouble.

"Until your mother starts her school," he went on.

"There's no child else to act the fool."

Mup leaned down, trying to see if any of the drawing remained. "It's all gone . . ."

She touched the wall where the drawing had been.

BAM, a firework of sadness exploded in her heart.

A darkness of guilt swamped her — a coldness of shame so strong and sharp and cruel that Mup fell to her knees.

"I'm sorry," she gasped. "I'm sorry."

Crow stepped back from her. "For what?" he asked suspiciously.

For what? Mup didn't know. She was just *sorry*. She was just *sad*.

She clung to the wall. Tears poured down her cheeks.

"I'm sorry for . . ." *For being happy.*

"I'm sorry for . . ." *For being a witch.*

"I'm sorry for letting Naomi into your bedroom!" she yelled.

Crow huffed. "Bedroom?" he asked flatly. "What bedroom?"

Mup looked up at him through her tears. "Mam . . . Mam and Dad gave you a lovely bedroom," she said. "Don't you like it?"

He stood looking down at her for a moment, his expression stony. Then he dragged Mup up by the scruff of her collar. Her hand broke contact with the wall, and she staggered back.

"I never asked anyone to give me a bedroom," said Crow. "I find my own places to sleep. I always have. I always will."

He walked stiffly away. Mup was left behind, her hand pressed to the hollowness in her heart. She stared down at the drying patch of wood where the drawing had been. It looked entirely innocent, but she backed away, afraid to touch it again.

At the end of the corridor, Crow paused. "Are you planning on staying there all day?" he snapped. "Because I fancied doing something more interesting with my time than gawping at a wall."

The Little Grey Girl

Crow marched ahead with determined independence. Mup wobbled along behind, her hand still pressed to her heart. She tried to figure out what had just happened and why she felt so bad. The original shock of sadness was fading, but the echo of it was still there: a guilty memory chewing at the edge of Mup's heart. As if she had done something very, very wrong many years ago. As if she had committed a terrible crime and had never made up for it.

They found Dad in the old guardroom—the one everyone used as a cloakroom. He was stamping snow from his boots and shaking snow from his hair. The door to the yard was open behind him, and dazzling light reflected from outside into the gloom.

Crow, with his usual enthusiasm for all things Dad,

rushed forward, his eyes bright with questions. He was obviously ready to resume their ongoing conversation in which he would quiz Dad for hours about the machines and inventions of the mundane world.

Mam, however, chose that moment to come in through the door, and Crow hesitated at the sight of her. He retreated to Mup's side and they loitered in the hall, she distracted, he wary, the two of them half hidden by the coats.

The adults had not seen them.

"Tipper enjoyed the snowballs," said Mam, her hands in her pockets.

"Yes." Dad smiled as he took off his coat. "He needed it. We all did." He glanced to the door as Fírinne stepped into view. "Where are the *clann*, Fírinne? I thought they were meant to sing the stones back into place today—rebuild the river wall against possible attack."

Fírinne stood pensively on the threshold. "They were meant to be here at dawn." She drummed her fingers on the door frame. She glanced at Mam. "I know you are expecting a delegation of Northlanders soon. I know we need to give them a good show of strength and unity if we're to win their trust. But I'm worried about my people."

Mam nodded. "Go," she said. "Find out what's wrong. I'll handle the Northlanders."

Without hesitation, Fírinne stretched, arched downwards, and became a cat. She shot off around the corner.

Dad blinked at the empty space where she'd only just been. "Not sure I'll ever get used to that." Then, as if what he was about to say might be a little touchy, he leaned across to Mam and muttered from the corner of his mouth: "Wouldn't it be quicker for her to fly? I mean, she could turn into a bird if she wanted to . . . right? The whole 'women are cats, men are birds' thing—that was just something your mother came up with?"

Mam shrugged helplessly. "I've no idea. They have been forced to live that way since they were born—maybe they can no longer do anything else."

"Huh," grunted Dad. "You'd think they'd be dying to at least try something new. I know I would." His eyes fell on Tipper, still rolling happily about in the snow. "At least our son has no trouble breaking the rules."

This dragged Mup's attention from the strange hollowness in her heart back to the reason she'd rushed down here in the first place. The little grey girl! Was Tipper out there on his own with her? Mup peered around her parents and out of the door. The girl was still there, her small figure barely discernible through the falling snow, all her attention resentfully focused on Tipper.

"Oh, *hello*, Mup," said Dad. "You missed a brilliant snowball fight." He peered to where Crow still lurked sootily behind the coats. "Hello, Crow," he whispered. "Have you been cleaning chimneys?"

Mam raised an eyebrow at Mup's clothes. "You're going outside in your jammies?"

"They're nice and warm," said Mup, her eyes slipping back to the little grey girl. *Don't you move*, she thought. *Stay away from my brother.*

"Still," said Dad. "A jacket wouldn't go amiss. And a hat, and boots. And gloves too."

Mup nodded, her attention still fixed on the girl.

"You too, Crow," said Mam. "Wrap up well. And don't leave the castle yard. Keep one eye on the sky and the other on the river. If you see anything strange or if someone sounds a warning, run inside immediately. Show me your lightning, Mup."

Crow winced as sparks blazed to life between Mup's fingers.

"Good girl," said Mam. "Don't be afraid to use that if you have to."

"You *won't* have to," said Dad quickly. "Because we're *safe* in the castle. Right, Stella?"

"Sure we are," said Mam. "Sure."

"*Since when,*" muttered Crow, "*has anyone good,*
Been safe around this neighbourhood?"

"The old queen's witches are gone now," Dad
assured him. "Aren't they, Stella?"

"Long gone," said Mam. "Far, far away."

"No, they're not," said Crow. "They're floating about
all over the place, aren't they? Climbing in windows.
Trailing muck on floors. Making themselves right at
home."

Mam crouched down in front of him. "Naomi
won't be allowed to harm you, Crow. I promise."

Crow stared hard at the floor. "People around here,"
he said, "are very fond of making promises they don't
keep."

Mam's cheeks flared pink. "Well . . ." She stood up.
"Well . . . I . . . I better go prepare for the next delegation."
She walked slowly off up the corridor, heavy in thought.

Mup rounded on Crow. "That was unfair! Mam's
doing her best."

"Who said I was talking about your mam?"

Mup deflated.

Dad's eyes hopped shrewdly between her and Crow.
"Tell you what," he said, "I quite fancy a hot chocolate.
Who wants some?"

"Me wants hot shockolate!" barked Tipper, barrelling in from the yard, scattering snow left and right.

Dad laughed. "Hot chocolate it is!"

Mup glanced outside. The grey girl had come to the mouth of the tunnel. She was glaring all around as if wondering where everyone had gone. Tipper bounced around the tiny guardroom, licking Dad's hands, trying to lick Crow's face, and generally being his usual happy nuisance. Mup didn't want him anywhere near that dark little figure that seemed to live in shadows.

"Tipper makes the best hot chocolate," she said.

Her little brother skidded to a stop, his brown eyes huge. "Is that true?" he barked.

Mup nodded solemnly. "I only like it when you make it."

"Daddy!" barked Tipper. "Me has to make the hot shockolate."

"As soon as the chocolate is made," said Mup, meeting her dad's eye as she took down her coat, "Crow and I will come up and drink it."

Dad smiled wryly at her. He obviously thought she and Crow were up to some game or another and needed to be rid of the baby so they could get on with it. "You'll wrap up warm?" Mup nodded. "And you'll stay in the yard?" She nodded again. "Okaaaay." Dad

86

herded Tipper up the corridor. "Let's go see how Badger is doing. I'd say a nice bowl of warm milk would do wonders for his arthritis."

"Me will make him warm milk!" barked Tipper. "I makes the best warm milk *and* hot shockolate . . ."

"You may need to be a boy for this job, Tip."

"Me will be a boy for when I needs fingers, and a dog for when I needs barks."

"Fair enough," said Dad.

Mup and Crow waited, motionless, until their happy voices faded.

Then Crow asked suspiciously, "What are you up to?"

Mup spun him about and pointed out of the door. "Look."

Crow lost his scowl at the sight of the little girl. "Oooh," he breathed. "She's *awful* dark."

He crept to the door, peering out.

"She's a ghost, isn't she, Crow? Though she doesn't look like any ghost I've ever met."

Indeed, the little girl had none of the shimmer Mup associated with ghosts. Now that she had stepped into the snow, she seemed even ashier and duller. Crow was right. She *was* dark—as if the place where she stood was dark, despite the swirling whiteness that filled the

87

space around her, despite the brightness of the ground and air.

As on the night before, her head was uncovered, her dress thin, her feet bare.

Aren't you cold? thought Mup. Without taking her eyes from the girl, she pulled on her jacket and her boots and her rabbit-eared hat. Before he could stop her, she wrapped a long scarf around Crow's head and neck. "Will you be warm enough, Crow?"

His voice came, muffled and grumpy, from the woolly depths. "I'm always warm. Stop giving me things I don't need."

Mup tutted. "Come on. Let's see if we can get closer without scaring her away."

Out in the castle yard, the marks from the snow fight were disappearing. The tracks from the visitors were long gone. The world was blank and cold, and silent. The grey girl, unaware of the two children creeping towards her, had crouched down and was scribbling crossly in the snow with her finger. Mup did not take her eyes off her as she and Crow drew closer.

She was *definitely* a ghost. Mup could see the stones of the wall through the transparency of her face. The bright snowflakes passed right through her thin body, dulling as they did so and swirling out the other side as what looked like ash. There was something terribly sad about the girl, and terribly lonely, and terribly angry. Mup began to feel sorry for her again, out here in her bare feet in the cold, carrying the dark with her.

Suddenly, the girl looked up.

Crow halted with a little *eep* of fear, but Mup kept creeping forward through the moving snow, her eyes locked now with those of the startled ghost.

Mup raised her hand. *It's OK. I won't hurt you.*

Though there were yards between them, the grey girl drew back, half in terror, it seemed, half in disgust that Mup might touch her.

Mup realized she was going to run. "Stop!" she cried.

The ghost shot backwards into the tunnel. She was gone so suddenly that she seemed to leave an image behind: her big, startled, outraged eyes—the only bright thing about her—staring for just a second before they disappeared like the rest of her. Mup was left peering into the blank darkness of the tunnel, snow falling all around her, and no trace of the girl.

"What is that?" whispered Mup, bending over the scramble of lines the girl had been scrawling. "Is it a dog?" She reached her hand, then withdrew it. The drawing was uncomfortably like the one that the butler

89

had been cleaning from the wall. Mup was afraid to touch it.

"It's a mess, is what it is," said Crow. He straightened his scarf, as if straightening his dignity. "Anyway, she's gone now. Too bad. We did our best. Can't say we didn't try. Hot chocolate?"

Ignoring him, Mup crept forward into the dark. She heard Crow groan in frustration. She heard him stamp about at the threshold of the light, then he followed her.

He pulled in close behind her as they edged deeper into the tunnel, groping their way along the wall. It was black as pitch, and colder even than it had been outside.

"This is where the witches brought us," Crow said. "When they put us underground."

The memory did something to his voice, his words coming out all shivery and thin.

Mup reached back, and Crow allowed her to take his hand.

She'd been in her animal form, trapped inside one of the witches' awful cloaks, when they had carried her down here. She remembered the cold closing in as they travelled deeper: the clink of the chains that had tethered Badger and Tipper, Crow's terrible silence after having discovered his dad was dead.

"I don't like the dark," said Crow. He said it a little accusingly, and Mup realized that he thought she could see. She couldn't, not when in her human form. If she transformed into her hare-shape she'd see everything clear as day, no matter how dark it was. But Crow wouldn't. He'd still be blind as a stone.

Mup came to a stop.

Crow froze at her side. "What is it?" he hissed. "Is she here?"

Why shouldn't I? she thought. *Why shouldn't I, if I can?*

Mup lifted her free hand. Gently, gently, she rubbed the tip of her thumb against the tips of her fingers. Gently, gently, the way she'd seen Crow's mother do—the way she'd seen other raggedy witches do.

"Crow," she said, "I don't want you to be angry."

He snatched his hand from hers. She felt him step back. Already, there was the faintest of glows emanating from Mup's fingertips, a dim and wavering blue light that showed stone walls and a low roof and an uneven floor. Outside this light was blackness. Still gently rubbing her thumb and fingers together, Mup raised her hand to reveal Crow's appalled face.

Crow's mother had been able to make the light solid; she had been able to leave portions of light behind. *Imagine if I could do that!* thought Mup in wonder. *Imagine!*

But so far this thin illumination was the best she could manage. It died altogether if she didn't keep moving her fingers. Still, Mup thought it was a brilliant thing to be able to do. She wanted Crow to think it was brilliant too. She grinned at him. "Now you can see!"

Crow scowled. "Couldn't you just light a candle, like normal folk?"

Disappointment stabbed her in the chest. "Crow, I'm only trying to help. Why do you have to be so rude?"

"Why do you have to be so *witchy*?"

"Witchy?" cried Mup. "Crow, *you can turn into a bird!*"

"That's not the same! Everyone does that!"

"Only because the queen *allowed* them to. Don't you understand, Crow? The only difference between you and a . . . a *raggedy* witch is that they were allowed to do things that you weren't. You don't have to live by those rules anymore. You can do whatever you want. You could probably even do *this* if you tried." Mup thrust out her glowing hand.

"I would *never* do that! I would *never* behave like one of her witches!"

"*There's nothing wrong with it!*" cried Mup, the light from her fingers flaring brightly. "Everyone here is a witch, Crow! Your dad was a witch. Your mam was a witch. You're probably even a—"

"I AM NOT A WITCH!" bellowed Crow. "HOW DARE YOU SAY I AM!"

Mup stepped back from him, her light fading. Crow's voice boomed away and away and away into the depths of the tunnel: *say I am . . . say I am . . . say I am . . .* Each echo more distant but no less angry, as if his rage were speeding away from them to some hiding place underground.

The dark around them seemed to grow thicker. Mup's light could barely illuminate it.

Crow's eyes glittered. "I don't like it here."

"I just want to see where the girl went," said Mup flatly. "You don't have to come."

She turned away from him, angry and hurt at his rejection of her, and continued deeper into the tunnel. After a moment, Crow scurried to catch up. Mup was glad to have him with her. She didn't admit to herself that he had no other choice—that without her Crow would be all alone in the dark.

"It's a . . . " Mup peered at the rapidly fading drawing on the wall. "I think it's a . . . frog?"

The drawing was terribly rough, with wobbling lines that didn't connect properly and were thick in some places and barely there in others. It was only the slight blobbiness of the shape and the smudged indication of a wide mouth—and were they eyes?—that made Mup suspect it was a frog. For all its ridiculousness, the drawing felt sad.

"Is it chalk?" whispered Mup. "It's more like dust or . . ."

Crow spoke reluctantly from behind her. "There's another one over here. A big one."

Mup turned, and the other drawing was revealed. Crow recoiled in horror. Mup slapped her hand to her mouth. "Oh," she said. "Oh, I feel sick."

She couldn't say why. All she knew was that the jumble of ashy scribbles clotted at the base of the wall made her stomach heave.

"They're dead," moaned Crow, backing to her side. "They're all dead."

Yes, thought Mup frantically. *Dead things. So many of them.* Birds, or fish, or some such fragile creatures, once vital and free, now jumbled together and piled high: all motionless and still, when once they had fluttered and leapt; all crammed into the dark, when once they had raised their faces to the sun.

"I don't like it," whispered Crow. "I don't like it, Mup. Please let's go."

"Yes." Mup was already backing away.

She kept herself between Crow and the drawings—needing to protect him from them somehow. She couldn't turn her back on them, and that was how she saw the face. Revealed as Mup retreated from the horrible scribbles at the base of the opposite wall, the face loomed from the dark as she swept her hand past it. It was huge—perhaps the span of Mup's arms spread wide—and much, much better drawn than any of the others.

She's practised this one, thought Mup. *It's maybe the first thing she ever tried to draw, and she's drawn it hundreds of times since.*

The drawing's eyes seemed to follow her as she stepped closer.

"It's crying," she said.

Fat tears the size of Mup's fist were drawn springing from the face's wide-open eyes and dripping from below its gaping, downturned mouth.

"It's crying," she said again, reaching, as if hypnotised, to touch one of the ashy tears. "But it's not sad, Crow. Can you feel that? It's not sad. It's . . ."

Realization hit Mup like a punch, just as her fingers touched the tears.

"It's angry," she growled, and the word "angry" was a feeling inside her: a red feeling, like a tide of fire rising to burn her throat.

A sound behind her made her turn. Crow was slumped against the far wall. He was crying, his chest heaving, his face drenched with tears. He gestured desperately at Mup. "Make it stop," he gasped. "Make it stop." Then he bent double, helpless under the power of his crying. He looked like he might *die* from crying.

Mup had no doubt what was to blame for Crow's tears.

Furious, she spun to the drawing. She scrubbed at the terrible face: smearing the ashy tears, the gaping mouth, the staring eyes into an unintelligible mess of dust. The tunnel plunged into darkness as her hands, otherwise occupied, lost their light. Behind her, a gasp and a croak and the stiff rush of wings signalled Crow turning to his bird form. He launched himself from the ground and flew for the mouth of the tunnel, which was just a coin of snow-light in the far distance.

Mup swept all around her, brushing and brushing away the dust. Not just the face but everything—all the unseen scribbles in the darkness, all the sickening scramble of horror and disgust. She was ablaze with anger. Crow was her *friend*. Mup *loved* him. How dare the ghost frighten him like that? How dare she reduce him to tears?

"How *dare* you!" Mup yelled.

She raised her hands, all rough with ashy remains, and aimed her fury at the darkness where the ghost lived. Mup was no longer interested in talking to the grey girl. She only wanted to destroy her, to make sure she never hurt Mup's friend again, to make sure she left Mup's family alone. Sparks arced from fingertip to ceiling to wall to floor. A wonderful rush of power flooded Mup's spine. She would bring it all down — all the great tons of rock — she'd bring it all down on top of itself.

A shrieking howl stopped her. A luminous pillar of light rose in the tunnel behind her.

Mup turned to see the little grey girl — bright and shining now in the darkness, her face a mask of horror and despair — rushing forwards with her hands outstretched.

Mup backed away, simultaneously shocked that she'd been about to bring the whole tunnel down on top of her head and frightened by the grey girl's sudden appearance. But the girl wasn't interested in Mup. She flew instead to the wall, to the smeared and unintelligible remains of her drawings, and she clutched at them, wailing.

Her distress killed the lightning at Mup's fingertips.

"I'm . . . I'm sorry," said Mup, still backing away. "They were hurting Crow . . ."

The girl, clinging to the wall, paused, panting — if a ghost could pant. She seemed to be gathering herself, gathering her understanding and her wits, her self-control. Then she turned to Mup. Her expression clenched down like a fist, her thin body coiled in on itself like wire. She was more cat than mouse all of a sudden, and she began to stalk forward, her expression all rage, after Mup.

Mup did not even hesitate. She just ran. Without bothering to make light, without bothering to fly, she raced for the tiny mouth of the tunnel, trying to distance herself from the little grey girl, trying to outrun the advancing tide of the girl's anger and sorrow and hate.

The Proper Shape of Things

Mup burst into the fresh air and ran all the way across the yard before she could stop. *What have I done?* she thought. *What have I done?* Gasping for breath, she spun and pressed her back to the door of the guardroom. She spread her fingers, lightning flashing to life as she waited for the girl to appear. The tunnel remained nothing but a blank hole in the base of the wall—the girl nowhere in sight.

The snow fell and fell, silently and relentlessly erasing Mup's footprints. With a shudder, she realized that if she had stayed any longer underground, there would have been no trace left to show where she and Crow had gone.

She glanced at the battlements, searching for Crow's shape against the wintry sky. She knew her friend had come outside. She'd seen him beating his way towards the light as she ran. But he was nowhere to be seen now. When she looked back down, the ghost was glaring at her from the mouth of the tunnel.

Hands raised in warning, Mup elbowed open the guardroom door and slipped inside. Shielding herself with the half-closed door, she watched as the grey girl emerged into the light.

The ghost took two uncertain steps. Then two steps more. She paused, hunched. As on the night Mup had first seen her, she seemed to be expecting something bad to happen.

Nothing did.

The ghost straightened. She met Mup's eyes. "Witchhh," she rasped.

Mup shook her head.

The grey girl nodded grimly. "Witchhh," she repeated, her voice rusty and unused. "Minionnn. Enforrrcer."

"I'm sorry I ruined your drawings," cried Mup. "But they were hurting my friend."

The word "friend" had a terrifying effect on the ghost. She seemed to swell. She seemed to surge with a whole new level of rage. Apparently incapable of containing such volcanic fury, she flung out her arms, threw back her head, and roared. No sound came, just a horrifying fountain of ash blasted from the girl's stretched mouth and billowed upwards before dissipating into the snowy air.

The grey girl swayed for a moment, as if the force of her anger had stunned her. Then she looked at Mup again from under her lowered brows. "Witches . . . don't . . . *deserve* . . . friends."

Without breaking eye contact, the ghost crouched and began furiously, feverishly drawing in the snow. Mup slammed the door on the sight of her, and ran.

The grey girl's jack-o'-lantern expression chased Mup down the corridor to the bottom of the staircase, where she launched herself into the air and flew.

She shot up the first staircases like a terrified rocket, her thoughts hammering in her ears: *What have I done? What have I done?* It was only when she turned onto the black-and-white corridor that she heard a terrible clamour — a wailing and a shouting — outside of her own panic. Her eyes widened as she realized it was coming from the floors above. It was coming from the family suite. She put on speed. Her surroundings blurred, fear for her family overcoming her fear for herself.

"Make way," a cold voice sounded behind her. Still

rocketing forward, Mup spun to see Naomi flying at tremendous speed up the corridor behind her. Dark clothes streaming, dark eyes intent, the witch gained on Mup in a trice, then shot past, the icy breeze of her passage tumbling Mup like a shuttlecock from the air.

Mup hit her head on the wall, rebounded, fell to the floor, rolled, and was on her feet and flying again all in one movement. She was following Naomi now, the two of them taking the corners in formation, heading for the terrible sounds above.

What is it? thought Mup. *Oh, what is it?* She could hear what sounded like Crow, cawing, cawing, and Tipper, barking. Her dad was shouting, and under it all, the quiet, barely substantial voice of Doctor Emberly wailed in distress.

The sitting-room door slammed open ahead of Naomi with a shocking boom, and then she and Mup were inside, part of a tumbling, chaotic, confusing scene.

A raven, huge and panicked, its great wings causing havoc, careened about the room, cawing in distress. Dad was trying to catch it, tumbling over furniture, tipping up tables. He shouted as he grappled the great strong bird, "It's OK, Tipper. It's OK."

Tipper? thought Mup.

As Dad held on, the raven's body changed in a

102

twisting, squirming, painful-looking manner and Dad was no longer holding a bird but a big, heavy, golden Labrador, whose weight carried them both to the ground. Tipper howled and kicked and scratched in panic until Dad had to let go of him and the chase began again.

"Tipper!" cried Mup. "Stop!"

But Tipper was beyond hearing. He sped round and round the room like a dog possessed. Past the fireplace, over the sofa, under the table—barking all the while and howling in fear.

The ghost of Doctor Emberly was pressed into the corner, almost one with the bookcases. He was shivering and crying. "I thought the enforcers were gone!" he cried. *"How can this be happening if they're gone?"*

Naomi watched from the doorway. She frowned as Tipper leapt for the sofa only to morph once again in that agonized way. Twisting, then tumbling into the air to become a raven, he flapped about in panic at the ceiling.

"Someone is punishing him," she murmured.

Doctor Emberly noticed her then, and he advanced from the bookcase, his tear-stained face even paler with distress. "Why must you still do these things?" he gasped. "Why can't you leave people alone?"

Naomi looked expressionlessly at him for a moment. Then she clawed her hand and hurled a gesture upwards to where the Tipper-raven scrabbled against the ceiling. An elastic globe of light flew from her fingers and encompassed him. He stilled immediately. A panting quiet fell on the room. In the stillness, Mup realized that someone had locked Badger in the library. He was snuffling at the door, scratching — too afraid to bark.

Dad, Emberly, and Mup all stood helplessly looking up at Tipper. He hung motionless in his iridescent bubble, still contorted in an attitude of panic: his raven's beak stretched wide, his round eyes bright with horror.

"Take him down," whispered Dad. "Please."

Still standing in the doorway, Naomi spiralled her finger.

The bubble drifted gently down, Tipper held within it.

Dad and Mup crouched over it, their hands poised — afraid to touch.

"Turn him back into himself," cried Mup. "Can't you turn him back?"

"But he's in his *proper shape* now, isn't he?" snarled Doctor Emberly, his distress turning to rage. "She's *done him a favour*. She's *made him normal*."

"This was not my doing," said Naomi.

"Of course it was. Who else would have done it? It's the enforcer's stock in trade, isn't it? It's what you people *do*."

"It is not my place to punish him for his aberrant nature."

Dad, still kneeling over the bubble where Tipper hung in frozen torment, stared at Naomi.

"Aberrant?" he whispered.

"The consequences for pursuing his differences are not mine to inflict."

Dad straightened. Mup had never seen such an expression on his usually jolly face.

"Consequences?" he snarled.

"What does she mean?" cried Mup. She spun to Naomi. "What have you done to Tipper?"

"Nothing but ease his distress."

"There is no distress in being *different*," howled Doctor Emberly, "except the distress caused by people like *you!*"

"That is not what I meant," said Naomi.

But Doctor Emberly was fizzing with rage and with a hurt that seemed to stretch back to long before today. "The old rules have crumbled. The queen's power is dispersed. Why must you still cling to this terrible torture?"

105

"Release my child," roared Dad, rising to his full height.

"I did not do this to him."

"Then why are you *here?*" cried Emberly.

"Because of the darkness." Naomi looked from him to Dad with the mildest expression of confusion. "Can't you feel it? It is so strong, like a tide seeping from underground."

She's right, thought Mup, looking all around as if her eyes had just been opened. *She's right.*

Everything looked the same: the messy, tumbled room, scattered papers, toppled chairs, poor Tipper twisted in his shining cage. But there was a new and crawling anger moving under the surface of it all. A sneaking, writhing darkness that Mup was only now aware of.

A tide seeping from underground, she thought. *From underground.*

From the dungeons!

Mup ran to the window, staring down through the snow, which was falling even more densely than before. In the yard, the grey girl had risen to her feet. A triumphant expression on her terrible face, she gazed up at Mup from her circle of scrawled and sprawling drawings. *There,* her expression seemed to say. *How do you like that?*

Mup slapped the window. *What have you done to my brother?*

The ghost just smiled.

"Dad," yelled Mup. "Come here! Come here and look at this!"

Dad did not look around at her. "Emberly, get my daughter out of here. Go find my wife." He advanced on Naomi. "You! Release my son!"

"Dad," cried Mup desperately. "Naomi didn't do this. Look! Look out of the window."

Down in the courtyard, the little girl—still deliberately looking at Mup—stamped her foot. The scrawled drawings of which she was the epicentre began to squirm. Wriggling, spasming, writhing on the ground like a mass of sleepy worms, they broke into individual pictures and crawled away from the girl's imperiously planted foot. As Mup watched, they burrowed down into the snow. Their progress was visible for a moment—as if a host of tiny animals were dashing away on their own secret business. Then there was no sign of them, just clean, clear snow where the hideous mess of drawing had been, and the little grey girl glaring triumphantly up at Mup from the pristine white as though to say, *There. Now I've got you. Now you'll be sorry.*

Mup spun to Dad. She recoiled at the shock of finding Doctor Emberly right beside her. His eyes were feverish, his transparent body distorting but not hiding the sight of Dad looming over Naomi. "Come now." Emberly's ghost-hand was firm on Mup's warm arm. "Come. Leave the witch to us. The days of them being allowed to torment people are over. Your poor brother shall soon be free."

Naomi spoke calmly to Dad. "If I release your son, he will be in pain."

"Not if you allow him to be *himself*!" screamed Emberly, rearing away from Mup in a sudden and uncontrollable surge of rage. "Why can't you see that? The worst pain we ever suffered was when your kind forced us into someone else's *shape*."

He shot towards Naomi, his whole being crackling with lightning. For the first time, Naomi's eyes widened with emotion. To Mup's astonishment, it was not fear but sympathy that she saw in the witch's face. As Doctor Emberly went to close his flashing hands around her head, Naomi raised a finger — all calmness — and he too was frozen, his rage and tears and untold years of pain confined, like Tipper, in an iridescent haze. Naomi flicked her finger and the doctor shot to the far side of the room to land in a heap, only his legs visible, his other half entirely disappeared into the bookcases.

Dad, his eyes wide with fear and determination, closed a hand around Naomi's neck and squeezed. "Stop hurting people," he growled.

Naomi allowed herself to lay a pale hand on his but did nothing more to resist.

"This . . . is not . . . my . . . doing," she managed.

"Dad!" cried Mup, rushing across and dragging at his unheeding arm. "Dad!"

Couldn't he see that Naomi could kill him nine times over?

Couldn't he tell that she was refusing to hurt him?

"Emberly!" snarled Dad. "Get up! Take my daughter to safety. Go get my wife."

The ghost pulled himself, groaning, from the confines of the bookcases. He staggered to his feet. He began limping towards Mup.

"Doctor Emberly," cried Mup, "you're wrong! I know the witches did terrible things to you. I know they did terrible things to everyone, but if you pause for just one moment, you'll be able to feel it. Naomi is telling the truth! This isn't her doing!"

But the ghost was inexorable, and Dad was a deafened wall of rage. The crawling sense of wrongness grew. It poured around poor Tipper in his cage and the stoic, choking witch. It gathered in glee around Emberly and Dad. Mup backed away from them. They weren't helping — they were making it worse. Dad shot out a hand to grab her. Emberly snatched at her. Mup evaded their grasp.

She darted from the room, slamming the door on the darkness within. Before Emberly could come through the wall or Dad could come through the door and catch her, she crossed the corridor, opened the window, and jumped out.

Friends

Mup shot upwards through the falling snow, a polka-dotted dash of colour against the stones of the castle walls. She had kicked the window shut before leaping into the air. She doubted anyone would guess she'd gone outside.

I need to get to Mam, she thought.

But the castle felt like it was alive with snakes, and she was afraid to go back in.

Up she flew, and up and up through the plummeting snow until she was among the turrets and gutters and the grim stone faces of the gargoyles. She paused, floating. The ground was a postage stamp of white below, the walls dropping sheer like cliffs.

The ears of her rabbit hat and the ends of her scarf whipped in the wind; the tails of her dressing gown flapped. A whiff of chimney smoke came to her on the pummelling breeze, and she thought, Crow.

She swooped ahead. Skimming the slopes of roofs and skirting snow-covered turrets, she followed the ever stronger scent of smoke until she came to a deep V formed by two sloping sides of roof. Within this soot-stained valley, the castle chimneys marched away in bristling rows. Mup was surprised at how many of them there were. The clever configuration of roofing kept them hidden from sight below, and kept the wind at bay. The snow fell quite peacefully here, mingling with the smoke, which rose undisturbed for several feet before being snatched across the rooftops and into the close grey sky.

It was warm and quiet, and Mup had no doubt that this was where Crow had made his sooty bed the night before. Sure enough, she found him at the far end of the valley, perched on a weather vane, which was mounted on the gable of the right-hand roof. His back was turned to her, and he was watching the sky.

Mup landed on the ridge tiles behind Crow. Snow dislodged from beneath her booted feet, rolled down the roof, and fell to a distant yard below. Her legs were shaky from the shock and fear of all that she'd just witnessed — but she was not afraid of the height.

It was so deceptively calm here: peaceful-looking.

Witches Borough stretched out on all sides: the frozen river, the miles of sleeping forest, the far-off hint of snowy fields. But over it all the castle loomed—dark as an infected tooth; sour with unresolved anger and hate.

Crow spun, startled, and Mup realized he had only now noticed her arrival. He covered his fright in a furious bristling of feathers. "What are you doing here?" he cawed. "This is my place! You can't just come up here!"

"Crow, something terrible—"

"Did you fly up here?" He looked around for footprints or other evidence to prove she'd walked or climbed. Finding none, he bristled even more. "So now you're a witch, you can go wherever you want, is that it? Like your mam and your grandma before you, you can just fly around and turn up wherever you please. Even if you're not invited? Even if you're not wanted?"

Mup ran the last few yards on the ridge tiles, hopped up, and wrapped her arms around the weather vane. Crow was perched on the north arm, his face now on a level with hers. Mup's arrival sent the two of them spinning, and they had to cling on tightly not to fall off.

"You're ruining my bedroom," howled Crow as they creaked round and round.

"Crow, something terrible has happened!"

"I don't care! This is my place! You can't just come up here!"

"Crow, the ghost has hurt Tipper!"

This stopped his raging like a bucket of water. "Little brother is hurt?"

"Oh, Crow, so badly!"

"We must go to him!"

Crow went to fly.

Mup grabbed him. "NO!"

They fell to the roof, a startled, fluttering, clinging bundle, sliding down to the perilous edge. Even as they tumbled, Crow tried to fly away—desperate, it seemed, to help Tipper.

"Wait!" cried Mup as her friend flapped and cawed. "You can't go back into the castle, Crow! There's something terrible happening in there! I'm . . . I'm scared to go inside!"

Crow stilled immediately, and they lay tangled at the edge of the plummeting drop, staring at each other in the falling snow.

"Scared?" whispered Crow, then, as if terrified into rhyme once again:

> *"What possibly could frighten you?*
>
> *You're the bravest person I ever knew."*

Mup released him. She tried to explain: Tipper twisted

in pain, Dad's hand squeezing Naomi's neck, Doctor Emberly transformed with rage. And of course the grey girl, her drawings crawling like a disease under the snow.

Crow shook himself, and all at once he was a boy.

They sat together at the edge of the roof, their legs dangling over the drop.

"*Little brother,*" breathed Crow.

"*Have you . . . have you asked help from your mother?*"

It was a desperate situation indeed if Crow was suggesting they turn to Mam for help.

"I don't know where she is."

"Well, *find* her, then!" he exclaimed. "Do your hare thing!"

Mup couldn't help it — through her beating panic and fear, she grinned. "My 'hare thing'? Wouldn't that be too 'witchy' for you, Crow?"

Crow just tutted and slapped his hand down onto the roof tiles as if to get her started.

Mup swallowed her grin and her panic and closed her eyes, searching inside for the calmness she needed. She took off her gloves and pressed her hands to the roof tiles, so cold beneath the snow. She waited for the network of paths to spread out beneath her palms, that vast, easy web by which the world made itself accessible to her. Nothing happened.

Crow watched her sideways from the corner of his bright eye.

"Well?" he said at last. "Did you find her?"

Mup opened her eyes. She climbed onto all fours. She called forth her hare-shape. Now she was looking down on clever, narrow paws instead of hands. Her whiskers trembled in the chill air. She burrowed down into the snow, shoulder deep for a hare, and pressed hard with the sensitive pads of her paws.

She squeezed her eyes shut. *Mam*, she thought. *Show me the way to Mam.*

The pathways opened reluctantly before her. Normally they sang out at her touch: each piece of the world merrily conversing with the next, sending information to and fro, round and back, with Mup at the heart of it all; the whole great conjoined web of existence opening out to inform and invite her — to guide her on her journey.

Now the paths opened only haltingly, piece by painful piece. Mup had to push every step of the way. She tried to remind each tile of the roof and beam of the ceiling and stone of the castle that they were not alone — that they were, in fact, snug neighbours who had lived side by side and conversant with each other for centuries. The tiles and beams and stones did not

116

want to know. After a very short communication, they withdrew into themselves and refused to talk.

Mup collapsed, gasping, into the snow.

"Are you all right?" asked Crow. "You looked like you were going to poo."

Mup shook her head. She tried again, pressing her paws to the roof tiles. The paths travelled no further than the empty attic below her and then stopped. Mup had to give up before her head exploded with the effort.

She sat up into her girl-shape, terrified. "I can't reach anyone, Crow."

"Is the ghost stopping you?"

"I don't think so. I think it's my grandmother's curse. I . . . I think it's the snow."

"The snow? What makes you think it's the snow?"

"It just feels like something my grandmother would do."

Mup shook her head, not sure how to explain.

The snow felt . . . It felt silencing. Like it was taking the living world and wrapping its mouth with bandages and burying it in a dark hole. It felt like the old queen.

The ghost? The ghost felt different. She felt like something that had been hidden and was now exposed, like a darkness seething up from some forgotten place. Like rage. If the snow was something being buried, the

117

girl was something else entirely rising from its grave.

"Crow?" asked Mup quietly. "What happened to you down in the tunnels?"

Crow hunched his shoulders. "I don't want to talk about that."

"You were crying. Down in the tunnels. I saw you."

Crow flared red. He began to bluster.

Mup pressed his arm, to reassure him that she wasn't making fun. "There's nothing wrong with crying, Crow," she said. "But I think it was the ghost who made you cry. Just like the butler this morning. I think . . . I think the ghost's drawings made you cry."

"Looking at them made me sad, that's all.

Those lonely dead things, on the wall . . ."

"They made me angry," whispered Mup.

Crow grinned at her. "Nothing wrong with being angry. It stops you from being sad." He gestured at his face. "See? Being angry dried my tears."

Mup smiled uncertainly at him. "Maybe you're right. But I'm starting to think that there's good angry and bad angry . . . and I don't like the kind of angry I felt in the tunnels, Crow. It didn't feel right." She looked down at her hands, remembering the tide of rage that had surged in her when she'd touched the drawings. "It was like I was a kettle someone had put on to boil and left until it blows up. It was like . . ." She softly slapped her hands together as if to trap her words between them. "I think that was what was wrong with Dad and Doctor Emberly. They were angry about Tipper . . . but then the anger twisted somehow and it wasn't about Tipper anymore. It was about something else."

Crow straightened, as if recognizing what she was saying. "That's how I felt! Down in the tunnels, I felt like I was crying someone else's tears." Crow put his hand over his heart. "I know what my own tears feel like, Mup. They're already too big. It's not fair to make me cry someone else's too."

"I need to find Mam, Crow," said Mup. "I need to warn her about the ghost. But . . ."

Mup saw again those revolting drawings burrowing away under the snow. She imagined them, right now, squirming through the stone and wood of the castle. Slithering in dark corners. Lying in wait. Where had the girl sent them? What did she mean them to do?

"I'm afraid," she whispered. "I'm afraid to go back inside."

Crow regarded her in silence for a moment. Then he toppled sideways from the edge of the roof. Mup cried out in huge alarm, but almost immediately Crow sailed back into sight below, his glossy wings spread, his crow-form dark and sleek against the distant ground. He looped back in a long graceful arc to land in front of her.

"You are my friend, Mup Taylor," he cawed. "Even if you did bring a witch into my bedroom. You are my friend because when bad things happen, you try and fix them. When folk are in trouble, you try and help them. You're the bravest person I know—even when you're scared—because you always try to do what's right."

Mup got to her feet at the edge of the roof, tears in her eyes. "Thank you, Crow."

"What is the right thing to do here?"

"I think . . . before we can do anything about this snow or my grandmother or anything else, we have to deal with the grey girl. To do that, I need to go back into the castle."

"Sounds like there's no time to waste,

So let's hop off and make some haste."

He sailed away again, his shadow hugging the blinding white of the roofs. Within moments, he'd dropped from sight. Mup leaned forward into midair, let the magic catch her, and swiftly followed.

Other People's Tears

They found an opened window and lowered themselves into the dim, dusty angles of an attic.

"Can you find your mother?" whispered Crow. "Now that we are out of the snow?"

Mup bent and pressed her bare hands to the floorboards. The pathways stirred with reluctance beneath her palms, travelling a little further than they had on the roof but not far enough to be of any use.

Mup shook her head. "We'll just have to look for her."

They crept together out of a little door and began a long descent down cold and empty passageways and narrow stairs, heading for the more opulent and populated areas of the castle.

It was silent for a long time. Silent and cold. Small

snow-crowded windows cast squares of speckled light, and Mup and Crow crept through them huddled like mice, waiting for the shadows to move, waiting for the grey girl to appear. She never did. They descended to a floor where the windows were tall, the floor polished marble. A sound began to grow around them, indistinct at first, then louder as they moved through the mostly empty halls.

"What is that noise?" whispered Crow.

"Someone is crying," said Mup.

And indeed that was what it sounded like: some poor isolated, lonely child, crying their heart out, their quiet sobs adrift and echoey up here in the emptiness.

"Hello?" cried Mup. "Where are you? Are you OK?"

"Wait!" Crow grabbed her arm. "What if it's the ghost?"

They shrank together. What if it *was* the ghost? Maybe they should creep the other way.

But, no! Mup straightened, remembering Tipper's suffering. No.

She wouldn't let the ghost hurt some other poor child.

She rushed forward, peering into empty rooms and calling loudly. "Hey. Hey, where are you? We can help!"

But it was not a child at all. When they finally found

the source of the crying, it was a big strong-shouldered liveryman, slumped on the floor by a window, too limp and sad to wipe his own tears.

"Mister?" Mup approached cautiously, her eyes darting about for the little grey girl. "Mister, are you OK?"

The man did not even lift his head from the windowsill.

Crow startled Mup by grabbing her shoulder. "Look!"

She followed his horrified gaze to the wall by the man's knee. Something fluttered there — a sickening, broken movement, as if a dying bird had found itself trapped somehow in the surface of the plaster. It was one of the grey girl's drawings.

"Mister!" cried Mup. "Come away from there!"

She grabbed the man's arm and tried to drag him away from the drawing.

He slithered to the floor, limp and heavy with sorrow.

"I'm sorry," he gasped. "I knew . . . I knew . . . all those years. And did nothing . . ." He shook his heavy head and pressed his wet face into the ground as Mup heaved and pulled on his arm, trying to get him moving. "I don't want to remember this . . . Don't make me remember . . ."

Crow yelled, "Mup, let him go! Look!"

The drawing on the wall had begun to grow. As Mup watched, tendrils spread out in a sniffing, seeking way, and it began to seep towards her.

"As soon as you touched him, it started to grow!

Let go of him, quickly! You need to let go!"

Mup dropped the man's arm. The drawing, disappointed, shivered back in on itself.

Crow began dragging Mup down the corridor.

"Leave him," he whispered. "We have to leave him."

The weeping man didn't even notice their departure. They left him where he was, crumpled in a heap, the black stain fluttering by his side.

They descended a staircase, clutching each other, not even pretending to be brave. The sounds of crying were louder now: a tide of unhappiness that rose to greet them when they were only halfway down the stairs. An entirely lonely, entirely hopeless sound.

I would die if I had to cry like that, thought Mup. *It would kill me.*

"I don't like castle people," whispered Crow.

"When others fought and died and fled,

They scraped and fawned and bowed their heads.

The way they watched us suffer and die,

I thought I'd want to hear them cry.

But I don't like this.

It feels wrong.

I wish . . . I wish it wasn't happening to them."

"Why are you rhyming, Crow? Is it because you're sad? Is it because you're scared?"

He looked at her with glittering eyes. "I don't feel safe," he whispered.

Mup suddenly realized that every time Crow had rhymed around her, it must have been for the same reason. Her heart became a little heavier, and she took his hand again and squeezed it, not knowing how to say sorry, or how to fix it for him.

She and Crow crept on, watching the shadowed walls for any squirm of movement. They came to a half-closed door. The sound of quiet sobbing could be heard within.

Crow pushed open the door.

It was a sewing room containing six large worktables. Each table had a high stool, and on each stool sat a tailor—three men and three women. Bits and pieces of black uniforms and half-constructed lace collars lay discarded around them. The tailors sat facing away from each other and wept into their hands. All around them—on the worktables and on the walls— the grey girl's drawings spasmed horribly.

One of the tailors lifted her head. To Mup's horror, the woman's face was crawling with drawings. "I'm sorry," she whispered. "I'm so sorry . . . We knew . . . all along we knew . . ." She choked and dropped her face once more into her hands, as if trying to hide from her distressing thoughts.

Crow went to comfort her. The drawings swarmed towards him across the fragment-scattered floor. Mup pulled him gently back. "We'll find Mam," she said. "She'll know what to do." They walked on, Mup towing Crow behind her, the tide of sobs emanating from many unseen places ahead and below.

"What if I start crying?" said Crow, fear heavy in his voice.

"There's nothing wrong with crying," muttered Mup.

"You know what I *mean*! If I start *that* kind of crying!"

He stopped walking, panicked by the tears which were suddenly pouring down his cheeks.

"Oh, Crow," whispered Mup. "Please don't be sad."

"But I *am* sad," he wailed. "I'm sad all the time! You keep hugging me and giving me things and wanting me to be happy, but I'm *not*!"

"I'm only trying to be nice, Crow. Why would me being nice make you sad?"

"*Because you're not my real family!* I miss *Sealgaire!* I miss my *cáirín!*"

Sealgaire, the *cáirín*: Crow's uncle and Crow's lovely little home, both of which Mup had destroyed in one single day. Guilt and shame surged painfully in Mup's heart, so strong and sudden that they brought her to her knees. Tears blinded her eyes.

"I'm so sorry, Crow! I never meant to hurt Sealgaire! I never meant to destroy your home!"

"I know! I don't blame you! *I'm just sad!*"

Crow fell to his knees at Mup's side, and the two of them knelt there, howling like babies.

Around them, the shadows fluttered gleefully as drawings crawled from every gap.

"WE HAVE TO STOP CRYING!" wailed Crow, and he held his breath, trying to force his tears back down to where they had come from.

But that's not fair, thought Mup, looking at Crow's swollen face, his desperate attempts to swallow his pain. Crow's feelings were real. He should be allowed to talk about them. He should be allowed to cry without being afraid the world would fall apart.

Mup dashed away her own selfish tears. She grabbed Crow's shoulders.

"Listen," she gasped. "It's OK to cry. I'm glad you

told me you feel sad. Of *course* you feel sad! You shouldn't have to hide how you feel, Crow. You lost everything. No matter what my family gives you, we won't ever be able to fix that."

"I know," he sobbed. "But . . . *but being sad makes me feel bad.*

I want to be happy for you and your dad."

Mup hugged him really hard. "Be happy when you're happy," she whispered fiercely. "And sad when you're sad. Don't worry about anything else."

"Mup," said Crow, his voice muffled by her hug. "I've decided. You can be a witch. I'll still love you."

Mup laughed. "I think I was always going to be a witch, Crow. Whether you let me or not. But I'm glad you love me anyway."

They both laughed through their tears. Still hugging each other and kneeling on the floor, they looked cautiously around. The drawings still surrounded them, sniffing and creeping, but in a confused way now, as if unsure of what direction they should go. Mup and Crow rose carefully to their feet.

"I think they've lost track of us," whispered Mup. "Maybe it's because we don't feel like crying any-more . . . or maybe it's because we helped each other?"

"But what if they make us cry? If they make us

cry in that way? What if we can't stop?"

"Then I'll . . . I'll make you angry," promised Mup. "I'll do something really dumb."

"Me too," said Crow. "If you get weepy, I'll . . . I'll pinch your nose."

They grinned at each other. Their eyes were very bright, but it was with the right kind of tears. They knew that only real friends would be able to do those things for each other. Only a real friend could hug you when you were sad without expecting your tears to stop just to please them. Only a real friend could help make your tears stop when you needed the sadness to go away. A friend might not be able to draw you a map, but they can always walk with you as you find your own way out of the dark.

Mup took Crow's hand. "Let's go."

Together, they stepped over the mess of drawings on the floor and continued on their way.

They passed weeping soldiers, a crying maid. They passed a closed room where someone sobbed, "I'm sorry . . . I'm sorry . . ." over and over again.

They descended a bright staircase to the halls below.

"This is where our rooms are!" cried Mup, recognizing the painted walls and tall arched windows.

She ran ahead, relieved that she would see Dad's familiar face and Tipper again at last.

Her hand was on the door handle when she recalled the scene she'd left: Doctor Emberly raging, Dad's grip on Naomi's unresisting neck, poor Tipper, contorted and trapped. Crow came to her side as she pushed open the door. The room was as she'd last seen it, all the scattered papers and tumbled chairs and tables messed about. Behind the library door, Badger whined and scratched. But there was no sign of Doctor Emberly, nor Naomi's tall, cool figure dressed in black.

Dad was there, though, slumped by the far wall. And Tipper was there, clasped in Dad's arms. Poor Tipper, frozen in that iridescent bubble, twisted in torment but so, so still.

Please let him be asleep in there, thought Mup. *Don't let him be awake and unable to move or scream or let us know that he hurts.*

She went to run forward, meaning to drop to her knees by Dad's side, but Crow grabbed her very hard by her wrist and pointed — dumb as a stone — to the floor at Dad's feet.

Oh no, thought Mup.

The floorboards were alive with drawings. The wall at Dad's back, even the glass of the window above his head, squirmed with ashy slashes and scrawls.

"Dad," whispered Mup.

He raised a tear-raw face to her. "What's wrong with me?" he gasped. "That poor woman. I nearly killed her. I nearly choked her to death . . ." He covered his face with his free hand. "How could I have? If Emberly hadn't pulled me off her . . . Oh, how could I have?"

"Dad!" Mup ran forward.

The drawings surged for her in glee.

Dad held up a hand to stop her. He lifted Tipper further from the seething floor. "There's . . . there's something wrong in this room, Mup. Stay . . . out there. Get . . ." He gasped and sobbed and banged his head against the wall until he found the control to carry on. "Get your mother . . . Tell her . . ." He began to cry again in earnest, tears pouring down his face. "Tell her I'm sorry I can't protect our kids . . ." Then, "NO! That's *not* what I want you to tell her. Tell her I'm *fighting hard* to protect our boy. Tell her I *need her help.* I don't . . . I don't think anyone should come in here . . . but I need her help. Can you do that for me, Mup?"

"Yes, Dad, but I don't know where Mam is!"

Dad tightened his arms around Tipper. He was on the edge of losing himself again. "I don't either," he sobbed. "You'll have to find her."

131

"We can do that, Dad!" cried Mup. "We can do that! Just hold on, OK?"

He nodded. The drawings were swarming around him — so many more of them than anywhere else, as if it had taken that many of them to wear him down, as if they'd had to work extra hard to worm their way through Dad's extraordinary good spirits.

"Hurry, Mup," he gasped. "I . . . I'm not doing well."

Crow cried out from their helpless position at the door:

"*Please, Dad-who-isn't-quite-my-dad,*
Please try hard not to be sad."

Dad smiled through his tears at Crow's earnest, anxious, sooty face. "I'm doing my best, Crow. But please . . . please hurry."

They closed the door, gently as if afraid to wake a sleeping baby, and ran on shaky legs away from the terrible scene. "Where are we going?" gasped Crow as they took yet another set of stairs. "What if we can't find her?"

"She was meeting another delegation," cried Mup, running, running, trying to ignore the sound of crying growing all around them, hardly even looking where she was going. "All the visitors come in from the river, right? We'll find her there!"

"Mup, you're going too fast! What if we meet the ghost! What if we run into some drawings!"

But they didn't meet the ghost and they didn't run into any drawings. Instead, they ran from top to bottom of that terrible, sighing, weeping place, sometimes with their hands over their ears, sometimes leaping over the bodies of people who were too sad to stand up. The only bright, moving, upright creatures in the whole afflicted castle, they ran until they were back where they'd started: dashing past the wainscotting where they'd seen the butler crying, racing down the lower passages to the guardroom, dashing past the coats and out into the snow.

Mam was sitting on the boat steps, snow gathering on her head and in her lap. She was all alone, gazing out to the river. The water and the far bank were invisible, and for one desperate moment, Mup thought they had disappeared. She skidded to her mam's side, staring out into a blank canvas, and then she saw through the moving air the barest suggestion of the far bank, the sketchiest hint of trees.

"It's got so foggy," whispered Crow. His voice made hardly a sound on the air.

Mam was motionless. Snow had piled against her in drifts. Mup swiped her face and swatted her shoulders clear of snow. Mam's skin was sparkling with frost, but when Mup grabbed her hands, Mam's brown eyes lifted to hers. There were teardrops frozen on her eyelashes, tears frozen in great clear crystals on her cheeks. "They never showed up," she said.

"Who, Mam?"

"The delegation. They never showed up. I don't know what to do anymore . . ."

"Mam, something bad is happening!"

"Yes. Something bad. People don't want to talk. All they want is to hurt each other, and to use me as a weapon. I don't want to hurt people, Mup . . . but maybe I *am* just a weapon . . . Maybe that's all I'm good for . . ."

Mam drifted off, her eyes turning back to the river. Mup shook her hard by the shoulders.

"Mam, you're not just a weapon. You're good! You listen to people! Trust yourself to do what's best!"

Mam didn't respond. The snow began to gather once more on her shoulders and hair.

"MAM!"

Mup started crying then—shaking her mam and crying very hard. Soon all she could do was cry. Her hands slipped from Mam's shoulders. She sank to the step at Mam's side. The cold world faded away for her.

It was quite comforting, really, to do nothing but kneel there. Someone else could bother with all the bad things for a while. Someone else could do the fighting and the arguing, and try and figure out what was right.

She leaned her head on Mam's shoulder and gave in.

Faintly, Mup could hear someone calling to her. She could vaguely feel someone shaking her arm, but her whole person was taken up with crying. She'd no room for anything else. It was all she wanted or was able to do.

But the noise would not leave her alone. It buzzed and buzzed at her as something shook and shook her.

Then came a blinding pain as someone tweaked her nose very hard.

Mup shot to her feet, yelling, "Ow! Crow! My nose!"

Crow was wrestling her away from where she had been sitting. He was stamping angrily on the ground. *Get away, get away from her.* There were drawings all over the ground, nibbling at Crow's feet, slithering and squirming to try and climb his legs.

Mup realized at once what had happened. She grabbed Crow around his waist.

Up, she thought desperately. *Up.*

She managed to lift the two of them into the air, scattering the clinging drawings as they rose. She wasn't far off the ground before Crow gathered his wits enough to become a raven. He flapped up out of her arms, and then they were both flying, safe above the ground, which crawled and skittered with dark, flat, erratically moving shapes. The shapes were gathering around Mam, tunnelling under the snow towards her, crawling up the steps at her feet.

"Mam!" called Mup. "Mam, move!"

But Mam didn't look up. She just sat motionless and isolated, pinned down by the cursed snow, infected with the ghost's drawings and her own self-doubt, unable to break free.

To Hunt a Ghost

"It's just you and me, Crow," said Mup. "We're the only ones left."

"A fat lot of good we're going to do,
With this great army of Me and You."

Crow huddled his knees up under his chin and stared dismally out across the snow-covered roofs and turrets. From where she stood on the edge of the roof, Mup could see right down into the yard. It looked peaceful and calm. Mam was a statue at the river's edge, gathering snow. From the floors and floors and floors of castle below there came the faintest, ghostliest sound of many people sobbing quietly. Or maybe Mup was imagining that.

"Where's Fírinne?" she muttered. "Where are the clann?"

Crow huffed. He was used to Clann'n Cheoil just running away from things. He would not be surprised at them not showing up in a time of need.

But Mup didn't believe that. She had seen the clann risk all in the battle with her grandmother. She had seen Fírinne's fierce loyalty and gratitude to Mam. They wouldn't abandon her—not unless something terrible had happened to them.

She walked to the far side of the roof, looking out across the forest. All was lost in white fog. Not even the thinnest thread of smoke was visible from where the clann had their camp. "Fírinne would be here if she could," she said. "It's the snow. Somehow, Grandma's curse is stopping them from getting back."

Reluctantly, Crow abandoned his watch over the yard. He came to stare out into the blank fog. After a moment's contemplation, he threw back his tousled head and crowed, loud and harsh. It was his people's cry for help. Even when the clann had been at their most impatient with Crow, Mup had seen them respond to this cry. It should have brought ravens wheeling from the sky; it should have brought cats swarming from the shadows: clann men and women, ready to protect one of their own.

Crow tried again, louder than before. His cry should

have carried far across the treetops. It should have rung from stone and tree. Instead, it batted into the fog, muffled and dead, and travelled no further than the edge of the roof. The snow-laden fog had eaten Crow's voice.

The nature of the old queen's curse made itself clear. They were cut off from the world.

"We're all on our own," whispered Crow. "No one's coming to help."

As if in response, the weeping below rose momentarily to a wail.

Mup and Crow looked down, listening. After a moment, the wail died down to a low, pulsing sob. They stood looking at their feet, wide-eyed. Then Mup straightened her hat.

"Well," she said. "At least we're not crying."

"I might start any minute."

Mup squeezed Crow's hand. "You cry all you want, Crow—as long as it's not the only thing you do."

She ran to the edge of the roof and jumped off.

"Where are you going?" yelled Crow. "No one knows how to break this kind of curse!"

"Crow," said Mup, floating back up, "I don't think there's too much we can do about Grandma's so-called 'curse.' If people are going to let a bit of snow and fog keep them apart, that's their business. Right now, I'm tired of being pushed around by a certain ashy little ghost and her horrible scribblings. I'm ready to give her a piece of my mind."

"I don't know what you hope to do." Crow fluttered down to land on Mup's head and peered with her down the ghost's tunnel. "It's obvious she's much stronger than you."

"Well, thanks a bunch," said Mup softly. She lifted her hand and rubbed her fingers together, casting dim and wavering light. There was nothing to be seen ahead—just the endless, downward-sloping tunnel, descending into the dark.

Careful not to touch the possibly drawing-infested ground, Mup floated forward.

Crow remained perched on her head. "What do you know about ghosts, anyway?" he whispered. "Nothing, I bet. You're going to drift on down into her lair, and then what? You're just going to clear your throat, tap her on the shoulder, and say, 'Ahem, excuse me, Spectral Miss. I'd very much like you to stop what you're doing and tip away off. This is my house now. You're not wanted.'"

"I don't talk like that, Crow."

"Like what?"

"Like that! All high and wavery and . . . posh. I've an ordinary voice! I . . ." Mup paused. "What's that?" she whispered.

Crow dug his claws into her hair. He crouched low against her head. "What's what where?"

"That light, up ahead."

"That's a ghost!" squeaked Crow, his claws positively burrowing into Mup's scalp.

"It's not her," said Mup. "It's too sparkly."

She let the light die at her fingers and drifted forward, squinting through the darkness at a thin, pale, hunched figure that illuminated an intersection of tunnels just ahead.

"Doctor Emberly!" she whispered in surprise. "What are you doing?"

The ghost turned his face to her. If a ghost could ever be described as white-lipped with fear, Doctor Emberly was just that. He clung to the wall as if barely holding himself together. "Why am I down here?" he moaned.

"Been asking myself the same question," said Crow, bobbing anxiously from side to side.

"I never wanted to be here again," moaned Emberly. Mup wasn't too sure that he'd even heard Crow. "Why am I down here?" he repeated. "Oh, please don't let me be here."

"Look at the wall by his hand," whispered Mup.

The stones were lit up by the ghost's desperately clinging fingers. They were alive with drawings, wheeling and crawling on the wall's surface wherever the ghost touched it.

"Doctor Emberly," said Mup gently. "Why don't you take my hand?"

"I'm so alone. I'm so alone. It's so dark."

"It'll be OK if you hold my hand, Doctor Emberly."

"I never did anyone any harm. I just liked a little music now and again, and a little poetry, and to be a goldfish instead of a raven. Is that a crime? To be a goldfish?"

"You bet your feathers it is," muttered Crow.

"Is that why they put you in jail?" asked Mup. "For being a goldfish?"

"I do so enjoy bubbles," whispered Doctor Emberly desolately.

"Doctor Emberly, why don't you hold my hand instead of the wall? You'll feel so much better. I promise."

Doctor Emberly turned his big eyes to Mup and seemed to see her for the first time. "Oh, little girl," he cried in great distress. "Oh, poor child! Have they thrown you here too?"

He took her hands, as if to comfort her, and Mup gently pulled him from the wall and up so that his feet were no longer touching the ground. The drawings scuttled away. The ghost's face instantly cleared. Mup smiled at him in the light cast by his luminous self.

"Feeling better?" she asked.

They held a whispered consultation in the middle of the corridor: Mup and Emberly floating together in the darkness, Crow perched on the top of Mup's head.

"I followed the witch underground," explained Emberly. "She's the cause of your poor brother's suffering, I have no doubt. As soon as your dear father released her throat, she fled — another proof of her guilt, you'll agree — and I pursued, of course. But I got a little . . . I got a little confused down here." He looked around in a haunted manner. "My memories got the better of me."

Mup squeezed his hand. He glanced sideways at her.

"Your father and mother are no doubt gathering their forces right now?" he asked hopefully. "I can leave the witch to them? I'd really very much like to not be here anymore."

"I'm afraid Crow and I are all there is, Doctor Emberly."

The ghost's polite hopefulness grew a little strained. "Do pardon me," he said. "I don't quite understand. You are all there is? You are all *what* is? You don't mean . . . ?"

"Doctor Emberly, could you give us some advice about ghosts?"

"You two infants?" he persisted. "You two *infants* are all they've sent to fight a witch? But she's one of *them!* Do you know what that means? Can they honestly expect two *infants* to get the better of one of *them!*"

"Doctor Emberly," insisted Mup, "we are not infants. And would you please forget about Naomi for a moment. It's *ghosts* we have to worry about. I need your advice about *ghosts*. Specifically, a little girl who —"

Doctor Emberly drew himself up with wounded pride. "My dear princess, I can assure you that none of your trouble has been brought about by ghosts. I know that your last experience of the recently dead was less than reassuring, but you must understand that the ghosts that rose to fight your grandmother's army were — well, let's say they were less than happy spirits. I can assure you that, for the most part, ghosts are perfectly *useful* and *decent*. We are kind, productive, informative, useful —"

"You've said 'useful' twice," observed Crow.

"Yes, but I'm simply making the point that our dear princess's recent experiences with the incorporeal may have coloured her opinion. Ghosts are invariably harmless, if not downright, um . . ."

"Useful?"

"Indeed! If not downright *useful*. If there is, in fact, a member of the disembodied community in the vicinity—which there isn't, because I was the only one to stay behind—I'm certain that when we *do* get to meet the little dear, she'll turn out to be the most charming sprite. A perfect playmate for your dear puppy—I mean, brother. A companion for yourself. A bright-eyed little scholar, even, to whom I can impart my encyclopaedic—"

"Doctor Emberly," said Mup. "Look at the wall behind you."

The ghost of Doctor Emberly eagerly followed the direction of Mup's gaze.

"Where?" he said. "Where? Show me the poor mite . . . Oh my," he said, recoiling from the dark drawings that crawled across the surface. "What are *they?*"

"I was hoping you'd be able to tell me."

"What disgusting things," said Emberly, peering at the drawings. "Quite slithering and rancid. These are obviously a witch's doing."

"They're not a witch's doing!" cried Mup. "They're *ghost* drawings. We'll prove it to you. Come with us." She gestured that he follow as she floated on down the tunnel.

"You're heading for the dungeons?" whispered Emberly.

"We think that's where she's gone," said Mup, turning back.

"The dungeons, though?" whispered the ghost. "Such terrible things happened there."

Mup floated back to him.

"We know," said Crow. "We were prisoners there too."

"But only for a little while," said Mup, thinking of poor Doctor Emberly's seventy-five-year incarceration. "And we didn't . . . you know, D-I-E here."

Doctor Emberly shuddered, staring at the drawings, which had begun to gather thickly again, as if attracted by his distress. "Oh, they're like bad dreams, aren't they? Or memories. I don't . . . I don't *like* my memories. I certainly don't want them scuttling about ready to leap out when I'm least prepared for them . . ."

Mup took his trembling hand. "It's OK, Doctor Emberly," she said. "Go back up top. Me and Crow will do this."

146

Her words brought the ghost's attention back to her. As if in wonder, he looked from her to Crow. "My dear children," he said, "there is one of the *queen's witches* prowling these tunnels. I will not, for one moment, countenance you going any further."

Mup dropped his hand. "Mmmhmm," she said. "Well. I'd like to see you stop us." She turned to go again, her hand raised to shed light. "Don't touch any walls, Doctor Emberly. And don't step on the ground either. The drawings are everywhere, and they're very poisonous." She recommenced her progress deeper into the tunnels, Crow vigilant on top of her head.

Doctor Emberly huffed and sputtered behind them. After a moment, he hurried to catch up.

He anxiously fell into place at their side. Mup smiled. Crow chattered his beak, and they went on, the way ahead a little brighter now that Emberly had added his light to theirs.

The Girl's Lair

The floor sloped down, and they floated past opened cells. Each tiny room was briefly lit by Mup's raised right hand as they passed, the shadows within leaping back to reveal stone walls, stone floors, emptiness. Cold seeped from each doorway. Shivering, they drew closer, Doctor Emberly holding Mup's free hand, Crow crouching on the top of her head.

They spoke in haunted, echoing whispers.

"What was it like?" asked Crow. "To live down here all those years?"

"I was not alive for very long," replied Emberly. "Though it felt an eternity at the time."

Mup tightened her grip on his hand. "But when you . . . ? You know . . . when you became a ghost, why didn't you just fly away?"

"Dear princess, I did not know that I could. I was just trapped. I was just alone."

"But when the ghosts followed Aunty out of the dungeons, there must have been hundreds of them. Thousands. Hadn't you ever talked to each other 'til then?"

Emberly shook his head. "It's hard to conceive, isn't it? So many years in the cold and dark, thinking I was alone. When all the time I was surrounded by fellow sufferers."

"When we found my dad," whispered Mup, "he wasn't even chained. It was the strangest thing. He was just sitting in the dark with the cell door open."

"Cell door?" Doctor Emberly halted as a memory stopped him in his tracks. "Oh, there *was* another prisoner. How could I have forgotten her?" He pressed his fingers to his temples. "I do think I may have gone very mad down here."

"What kind of prisoner?" asked Mup.

He turned astonished eyes to her. "Why, she was a little girl."

Mup leapt in excitement. "What kind of little girl? Dark? Grey? Ashy?"

"Twisty? Dirty? Nasty?" added Crow. "Black eyes full of hate?"

"Oh no," insisted Doctor Emberly. "Not at *all*. Such

a kind, gentle little child. She would creep to my door after the witches . . ." The ghost shrank a little in remembering. "After the witches had finished with me for the day," he whispered.

"This was when you were still alive?" asked Mup.

"That terrible tortured time."

"Was she a ghost?"

"You know, looking back on it, I think she was. I was in such pain at the time, it hardly registered with me. But she cannot be who you describe. She was lovely — such a comfort to me in my extremity."

Doctor Emberly startled them both by howling in guilt. "Oh, how could I have forgotten her? How *could* I?" He flung himself back, clutching his head.

Mup pulled him upright before he could tumble into the treacherous wall. "It's OK, Doctor Emberly. Please don't cry."

"But my poor little friend. I used to be so frightened for her — all alone, creeping from cell to cell. She was the only light I would ever see. She told me she visited all the prisoners, taking from us all. She told me never to worry. She told me she had a place to hide. She said . . . she said she was building a friend to protect her . . ." He clasped his hands, silently remembering.

"Building a *friend*?" asked Crow.

"You said she used to take something from you?" whispered Mup. "What did she take?"

"Why, she would take my pain, dear princess. She would take my pain, and my anger too, and all my despair. For the shortest while after she had gone, I would be content . . . until the witches returned and the whole terrible business started again."

"She took your *pain*?"

"She would just . . . call it. She'd stand at the door of my cell—she never came any further than the doorway—and she'd ask my name. She'd say . . . she'd say, 'I will never forget you, Erasmus Emberly.' Then she would *call* as if to a little dog, and all my pain would leave me. It would just *leave* me. Sometimes I would see . . ." Emberly shook his head. "But no, that can't be right. I must have imagined that."

"What would you see?" whispered Mup.

"Sometimes I thought I could *see* my pain leaving me. In the light cast by her feet on the stones, I'd see a kind of darkness running to the girl. She'd walk away with it scampering at her heel. When I died, she stopped visiting. I suppose she forgot me in the end. As I forgot her."

"Did she ever draw things?"

"No!" snapped Emberly. "I *told* you. She was a

sweet thing. A *lovely* child. I will not have you connect her in any way to those dreadful scrawlings. They are undoubtedly a witch's doing." Appalled at himself, Emberly slapped his bright hand to his mouth. "Oh, I'm so sorry for shouting at you. Forgive me. Please. I do not like to remember this. It makes me . . ."

"It's OK, Doctor Emberly," said Mup gently. "I think you're very brave."

Crow bobbed and muttered on her head:

"Brave or not, we should press on.

We've stood round here far too long."

They once again commenced their wary progress past many tiny cells. The walls here were free of the crawling drawings. Mup supposed they had left in search of easier prey.

Or perhaps, she thought, *we've gone too deep now.* Perhaps those drawings were only meant for the living denizens of the castle above—those who would be most hurt and crippled by the memories they invoked. Perhaps the little grey girl never expected anyone to journey this far into the dark.

On and on, past gaping doorways and branching tunnels. Then, all at once, there were no more doors; there was just a blank-walled corridor, which spiralled down and down, deeper underground. *Who would the witches have brought here?* thought Mup, gazing into the mouth of the tunnel. *Where would they have kept them if there are no cells?*

Down into the steeply sloping passageway they went, eyes bulging at the darkness.

"Look," whispered Crow.

Mup raised her hand. Drawings filled the walls of the narrow tunnel ahead; they filled the ceiling; they filled the floor. Smudged at first, but growing clearer as Mup and Crow advanced: these drawings were not living, as the ones above had been, but they had their own power, the jumbled lines all tangled and oppressed. Mup's heart crawled slowly into her throat as she imagined the grey girl down here all alone in the dark, her grim face set, drawing, drawing, drawing these scrambled, frenzied things.

The air was thickening. Mup began to feel breathless and pressed upon. The darkness began to feel like a pressure against the fragile light in her hand. On her head, Crow made a small noise, and she realized he was crying.

He protested when she tried to look up at him. "It's only tears," he croaked. "They're coming on their own without my meaning them. You're the same. So is Emberly."

She touched her fingers to her face. They came away

wet. Emberly's face was drenched in luminous tears. *How dare she,* thought Mup. *How dare she make us cry without us wanting to?* Her heart began to burn like a coal inside her. She welcomed the rage and swiped away the tears.

"She's close now, isn't she?" whispered Crow.

Mup nodded.

Ahead of them, the tunnel spiralled around another bend. Someone was muttering down there — a feverish sound. Getting closer, Mup saw a foggy light illuminating the wall where it curved out of sight. She dropped her hand, allowing her own light to extinguish. Crow gasped. All around them, the drawings began to glow. They didn't cast enough light to see by — indeed, they made the walls and ceiling and floor seem to warp and swim so it was difficult to know which way to turn without tripping or falling or banging into something. But the light ahead shone like a beacon, and Mup floated towards it, hands clenched, heart pounding with anger and sadness and fear.

The grey girl did not notice them as they came around the bend. She was too busy, and too tormented. All her concentration was occupied in drawing. Scrawling with her finger directly onto the stone, without chalk or pencil or paint — just the ashy residue of her frantically moving hands — she was floating halfway up the wall in front of them, feverishly occupied in filling every blank spot with scrambled, unreadable pictures.

The drawing seemed to give her no pleasure. In fact, it seemed to give her some pain, and Mup's heart twisted at the torment on the smaller girl's face. *Why can't they leave her alone?* she thought. *She did nothing to them. It's not her fault they died here. Why can't —?*

As if to silence a distressing voice, the grey girl cried out and slapped the side of her own head. Mup reeled back, the sudden intrusion of angry, alien thoughts vanishing from her mind. The grey girl clung to the wall a moment, gathering herself. Then she stretched high above her and, without looking, her eyes tight shut, she swept her arm down and around into the smooth, clean line of a circle. Then, with the same smooth, effortless sweeps of line, she drew the eyes, the nose, the downturned mouth of the crying face.

Crow groaned with horror and shuddered a sob. Mup clamped down hard on her own tears. The air became thick with sadness. The drawing seemed to give the grey girl some relief from her frantic pain, though. She lovingly drew each spouting tear. Then she just floated there a moment, with her forehead pressed to the ashy lines of the angry-sad face, as if its proximity comforted her.

155

A familiar howl came echoing from the darkness ahead. Mup recognized the sound of a huge dog, trapped and alone. The little girl stroked the crying face, as if she were easing the dog's pain.

Shh, her gesture seemed to say. Shhh.

Mup had almost forgotten Doctor Emberly until he pushed gently past. All his attention was fixed on the little grey girl. "My poor child," he whispered. "My poor friend."

To Mup's alarm, he drifted forward, his hand lifted to the little girl, who clung now like a startled bat on the ceiling, watching him approach.

"My dearest girl," he said. "Don't you remember me?"

Mup saw the girl's expression change from outrage to curiosity. Her ashy head tilted as she seemingly fought to recollect.

"You were so kind to me," said Doctor Emberly.

The girl scuttled forward. Stretching down from the ceiling, she twisted her head and peered into Emberly's gentle face. She seemed to be confirming something for herself—searching through her mind. Then her face cleared. She nodded. She floated down from the ceiling and crouched by the far wall. She gestured in invitation, and Emberly crouched with her. Mup and Crow seemed not to exist for her. She took Emberly's luminous hand in her own darker one and pressed his finger to an area of particularly dense scribbles.

She looked up at him, a smile incongruous on her pinched face.

Emberly reluctantly shook his head. "I'm so sorry," he whispered. "I don't understand."

The girl frowned. She impatiently scrubbed the area of scribbles clear. Then, painfully, carefully, she redrew one of them. Mup and Crow crept perilously close to see. It was not a good drawing, and it was very small, but without the confusion of others blurring it, it was clear to see.

It was a goldfish, a stream of tiny bubbles climbing from its mouth.

"Errr-aaas-musss," hissed the little girl.

Doctor Emberly sobbed and slumped to his knees.

The little girl petted him fondly on his shoulder. "Errr-aaas-musss," she repeated.

"She remembers you," whispered Mup.

"Can't you see?" cried Emberly. "Can't you see? She's remembered us all!"

He swept his arm to the jumbled scrawls crowding the walls, and suddenly, Mup understood what they were. Layers and layers and layers of drawings—made indecipherable by their very quantity—layers and layers and layers of tiny birds, tiny fish, tiny dogs, tiny rabbits: all the forbidden animals, all the prohibited shapes, all the lives lost and forgotten down in the dark at the hands of her grandmother's minions, remembered here and in the only way she knew how, by this one small child.

"And I wiped them out," whispered Mup. "No wonder she was so angry."

Crow flew to the ground and rose into his boy-shape, his eyes roaming the walls. "My dad! Is he here?"

The girl surged to her feet at his cry. She spread her arms as if to shield the kneeling ghost from Crow, whom she only then seemed to notice. But soon she realized that Crow was searching the walls, and she tilted her head in that listening way of hers, trying to understand what he was saying.

"Toraí," cried Crow, searching and searching the indecipherable scribblings. "His name was Toraí. Toraí Drummaker of *Clann'n Cheoil*. Is he here? Do you have him?"

Expression clearing, the ghost drifted forward. She took Crow's hand. She led him to a different part of the wall. She pointed. He shook his head, not seeing. She cleared a space, and again, carefully, painfully, she created a drawing from the ashes of her own hand. A tiny, tiny, rough drawing, it was meaningless to anyone else. But Crow wept when he saw it, and he nodded and he said, "Yes. Yes . . . Dad."

The ghost gently patted his shoulder. "Toooreeee."

Mup gazed at the sooty mark that was all that remained of Crow's father. *That could have been my dad,* she thought. *That could have been all that was left of him.*

A terrible howl rose again in the not too distant darkness: the great dog, baying in warning. Mup heard the faint sound of huge nails clawing on stone. It sounded like the dog was trapped behind a wall. Like it was scraping to get free.

The grey girl stepped away from Crow, alerted by the sound. She spun to scan her surroundings, and in doing so, she saw Mup for the very first time. The girl's eyes widened in angry recognition. She clawed her hands in rage.

"I didn't know!" cried Mup. "I didn't know what your drawings were! I'd never have destroyed them if I'd known!"

But the grey girl was advancing, her hands raised in vengeance. Mup felt the sorrow and fear of the girl's power rise from the walls.

"WAIT!" cried Mup. "LET ME EXPLAIN!"

Behind the girl, Crow scrambled backwards as drawings swarmed down from the walls.

Emberly struggled to his feet. "My dear girl! My dear girl, listen!" But his cries were drowned in the distant howling of the dog and in the vengeful roar that now poured from the girl's distorted mouth.

She advanced on Mup. Mup backed away, her own hands raised in a warning that Mup no longer wanted to act upon. "Listen to me!" she cried. "LISTEN!"

A bolt of green light shot from behind Mup.

The grey girl was thrown backwards by it and slammed against the far wall.

"That creature is no longer capable of reason," gasped a rough voice. "Back away from it." It was Naomi, staggering down the tunnel from above, dishevelled and strained as Mup had never seen her. Her face was blotched with crying, her expression twisted with barely maintained resolve. "Back away from it," she gasped again to Mup. "Hurry, while I am still capable of helping you."

At the sight of the raggedy witch, the little grey girl rose in a tower of fury and fear. She glared from Naomi to Mup. I knew it, her expression said. I knew you were one of them! Behind her, the dog's baying lifted to terrible heights, and the ghost threw back her head and howled in reply.

Naomi advanced with raised hands. Crow shot past her to Mup's side.

"Doctor!" Naomi called harshly to Emberly. "Run."

But Emberly was still kneeling by the wall, gazing up in sympathy at the boiling creature that used to be his friend. "Poor child," he whispered. "Poor child."

Naomi made a grab for him. The grey girl — obviously afraid for Emberly's safety — swooped between them. She roared in Naomi's face, her intent unmistakable. *LEAVE HIM ALONE!* The witch's hair flew back in the blast; the witch's eyes clenched shut. In that brief moment, the grey girl snatched Doctor Emberly from the stones and shot off with him down the tunnel.

The air shuttered to blindness. Mup was left stunned in the dark.

Eventually, Crow's thready voice ventured a question: "Is . . . is everyone dead?"

Mup lifted her hand and shed some light. Emberly was gone. Naomi was an untidy crumple on the ground. All around them, the drawings remained still and dull. Mup rose to her feet, avoiding touching them. She set off deeper into the tunnel. Crow grimly followed.

Naomi stirred as they limped past. "Where are you going?"

"To rescue Doctor Emberly," said Mup. "There's no way we're leaving him here."

A Safe Place

They did not have far to walk. The tunnel ended in a
dead end, a stark full stop to its relentless downward
spiral. The walls and ceiling on the way down had been
thickly encrusted with the little grey girl's unintelligible
scribbles. But the wall that now barred their way was
clean except for one drawing: the now familiar crying
face. It filled the entire space of the wall, menacing in
the light cast by Mup's upraised hand.

Naomi limped up behind them. "We cannot be
here. No one comes here. Not even named disciples of
the queen."

Crow laid his fingers on the wall. "What is this?
What's behind it?"

"I would only be guessing what it is. Repeating old
stories that may not be true."

What is it?" demanded Mup.

"It is from before my time," said the witch, almost defensively. "Probably long before even your grandmother's time."

Mup laid her ear to the stones. Silence greeted her, and then the very faint scrabble of claws on the far side. Mup jerked back. Naomi stared at her from the darkness, her pale face and wide dark eyes barely illuminated by Mup's raised hand.

"Tell me what this is," whispered Mup.

"It is an oubliette."

"Oubliette . . ." Crow mouthed the word without comprehension.

"A room with no door," said Naomi. "A room where people were put and forgotten and left to die." She lifted her finger, pointing to some vague place overhead. "They would have been lowered in from above. Through a hole in the ground."

"Like into a well?" gasped Mup.

The witch nodded; even she seemed green at the thought.

Once again, Mup pressed her ear to the wall. "Doctor Emberly?" she whispered. "Are you in there?"

Once again came the scrabbling of claws. Listening carefully, Mup thought she could hear the heavy, snuffling breath of a huge dog working its way up and down, up and down, as if patrolling the short length of the wall.

She built a friend to protect her, thought Mup. *She found a place to hide.*

Mup heard the voice of Doctor Emberly, muffled under the snuffling and the scrabbling. "Oh, please. It is so dark. I cannot stand it. Please, please won't you set me free?"

"Hey!" shouted Mup. "Hey, ghost girl!"

Crow moaned softly and half gestured as if to silence her. But Mup was not afraid to be angry now, not when the anger was entirely her own, not when there was something so awful to be angry about. She banged the wall with the palm of her hand. "Hey! Doctor Emberly doesn't want to be in there! Let him out."

Only the snuffling of the dog and Doctor Emberly's muffled sobs answered her.

Mup pressed her hands to the wall and concentrated very hard. *Move,* she told the reluctant stones. *Move.* She heard herself make a strained little noise. Light seeped from her fingertips and was soaked up by the wall. Suddenly, Crow leapt to her side, pushing. They made no impression at all on the unalterable structure of the wall.

"Don't push, Crow," said Mup. "Sing. That's what your

people do, isn't it? Like when the clann dismantled the river wall? Sing!"

Crow's eyes opened wide with fear. He glanced at the raggedy witch, who stared palely at him from the dark. "I'm not allowed," he whispered.

"Says who? My nan? She's gone, Crow. Stop living by her rules! Help me! Sing!"

Naomi's eyes roamed the wall. "There is a lot of power behind that wall. I do not think—"

"Doctor Emberly is behind that wall!" cried Mup. "He died down here! He only just escaped from here. I'm not abandoning him. Crow, you said you loved me even if I was a witch. You said you'd be my friend. Well, you need to be your own friend too. Let yourself be magic, Crow. Be proud of what you are! Sing!"

With that, Mup spun to press her hands to the stones again. Again she urged her magic into them. *Move. Move.* Suddenly Crow was at her side, his fingers spread on the wall. But he wasn't pushing. Instead, he seemed to be thinking, trying hard to remember. Mup continued to press and press her magic into the stones. Her heart jolted as one of them shifted. *Yes!*

Then a sweet thread of sound rose up beside her. Oh so sweet that Mup had to stop for a moment just to listen.

Crow was singing.

Standing there in the darkness, with a witch looming behind and the ghost lurking ahead, Crow released a song like nothing Mup had ever heard: clearer and brighter and purer than any previously sung by his people.

Mup felt the stones grate beneath her hand.

"Yes, Crow! Keep singing!"

She pressed her palms to the wall again.

Magic seeped from her splayed fingers, runnelling out into the seams and cracks.

The wall began to shake. *We're doing it,* she thought. *We're doing it!*

Behind the quaking stones, something growled, low and dangerous. The wall bulged outwards, as if pressed from within.

"Step back," cried Naomi.

"We're not leaving him!"

"Step back, you fools!"

The wall exploded.

Bones and skulls shot from the crowded darkness, shattering to powder on the tunnel walls.

Centuries of stale dust rushed the frigid air.

Mup and Crow were flung backwards.

Naomi lunged past them, her hands flashing. A

great bubble of power blasted from her fingertips. The exploding wall and the ravenous beast that had begun to burst from behind it froze and hung quivering in midair.

"RUN!" screamed Naomi, her arms up to contain the beast. "RUN!"

Stunned, Mup and Crow were only able to stagger and fall, choking on the rancid dust.

At the back of the oubliette, the pallid light of Doctor Emberly rose to sight.

"Hurry!" cried Naomi. "For grace, hurry, man! I cannot long hold this creature at bay."

The doctor ran towards her. As he crossed the hidden room, his ghost-light illuminated mountains of dried bones, seeping walls, the twisted shape of the huge clawed creature that Naomi's magic held suspended overhead.

Emberly spared Naomi a wide-eyed look as he passed. "What of you?"

She glanced once into his luminous face. "I deserve no better than this," she said, and she returned her attention to holding the vast creature motionless in the air above her.

Mup struggled to sit; her fingers sparked with weak light as she tried to add her magic to Naomi's. Far back, amongst heaps of skeletons, the little grey girl stepped into view. She regarded the fierce, suspended shape of her animal friend. She regarded the straining witch that held it in place. For the second time in perhaps centuries, her scratchy, unused voice made a sentence.

"You . . . have . . . broken the wall . . ." She smiled. "Now . . . he is . . . free . . ."

"RUN!" screamed Naomi again.

Emberly swooped past her; all that was behind him fell into shadow as he lifted Crow in one spectral arm.

"I can . . . fight . . ." Mup coughed. "I can . . ."

Ignoring this, Emberly scooped her up in his other arm and ran. Mup joggled against his luminous shoulder for a moment, limp as a stunned sack, staring back at Naomi.

Arms spread, the witch was silhouetted against the grey girl's light, the girl's creature a snarling mass above both their heads. The grey girl walked towards the witch, that cold smile on her ashy face. She lifted a small finger and pointed.

The creature fell.

It closed its many jaws.

Naomi screamed and screamed.

At the top of the tunnel, Emberly dropped Mup and Crow and they all ran, hands clasped over their ears, eyes streaming tears. Naomi had won them this precious time; she had sacrificed herself for this, and they did not waste her gift. Up the spiralled corridors they ran, past the chilly doorless cells—running, running from the terrible screams, until Naomi's cries abruptly ended and silence fell like a hammer blow on their ears.

They turned as one, panting.

"She . . . she saved us," said Emberly.

He stepped forward, perhaps thinking to run back for Naomi.

Mup gripped his arm. "Listen."

Other sounds were coming now from the echoing tunnels below. Sounds—half heard, half imagined—that shivered the heart in Mup's chest. Sounds that had Crow plucking frantically at her sleeve and had Emberly silently stepping backwards.

A distant scrabble of claws on stone, the faintest snuffling of a huge dog's breath, and then—far below them—the raging, trumpeting howl of a hound that has caught the scent of prey and has been released at last to the hunt.

The Rage Dog Hunts

They flew through tunnels and twisting paths, pursued by the rage dog's baying.

"Where are we?" panted Crow. "Did we take a wrong turn?"

Somewhere they must have, but they just kept flying anyway, Emberly and Crow blindly following Mup, zooming around corners and always taking the upwards path.

They burst from an unexpected exit into blinding light and waist-deep snow. They were in the little garden onto which Mup and Crow and Tipper had looked down only the morning previously. Walls rose up on all sides, filled with graceful windows. The sky was a small stamp of grey above, emptying snow onto the muffled shapes of trees, flowerbeds, statues, and paths.

The stillness and the quiet stunned them for a moment. Then Mup spun to face the tunnel mouth. They backed away from it, leaving a channel in the snow, watching the darkness and listening.

There was only silence below.

"Maybe . . ." said Mup, "maybe it can't come up into the air?"

But then a terrible noise rose up in the building behind them.

Somewhere on the basement floor people were screaming.

Emberly pointed to a window very close to the ground on the other side of the garden. A terrified face appeared at the glass there. They hammered desperately, trying to get out. Before Mup could do anything, the person looked behind them, as if hearing a noise, then dropped and fled. Mup could see them briefly in window after window as they ran what must have been a long semi-underground passageway. At the last window, the person looked briefly behind them again, and then fled into the depths of the building.

Crow's desperate grip on her arm brought Mup's attention back to the first window. A huge creature filled the passageway there, all jaw and milky eye, all massive roiling body. Snuffling blindly forward, it scampered from floor to wall to ceiling with astonishing agility. Now and then it lifted its head in a piercing howl.

Behind it, the grey girl stalked—confident now, after centuries of hiding—ready to avenge herself for untold magnitudes of anguish and hurt.

"Oh, my dear," whispered Emberly. "Oh, dear girl, no. This isn't right." He began to wade through the snow. Then, seeming to remember he had no need of such clumsy locomotion, he rose into the air and shot forwards.

"What are you doing?" cried Mup. "Stop!"

Emberly had already disappeared into the far wall. He appeared in the corridor ahead of the rage dog, his hands up as if to stop its progress. Mup and Crow heard the growl from where they stood. The dog went to surge forward. The little girl stilled it with a word—her voice inaudible from where Mup stood. Emberly advanced on her, his hands out in supplication, his lips moving in rapid speech.

Head tilted, the girl listened carefully to what he had to say. Then she nodded in solemn understanding. She pointed her finger. Doctor Emberly rose into the air as if lifted against his will. The little girl twisted her hand and he floated towards her.

Guiding Doctor Emberly's progress through the air, the little grey girl drew him over the panting, curious head of her dog. It snuffled him as he passed, but otherwise let him go.

The grey girl brought Emberly safely down by her side. He spoke again, pleading. The grey girl patted him kindly on his arm, and then she and her dog continued their relentless hunt, paying no heed as Emberly called to them from behind. Girl and dog soon disappeared from sight, and the screams started again, working their way up onto the next floor.

"Dad," whispered Mup, looking to the upper floors. "Tipper."

She and Crow launched themselves into the air.

"Dad!" Mup hammered a window many storeys up.

Crow fluttered from ledge to ledge, peering inside. "Is this even the right floor?"

"I don't know, Crow! They all look the same on this side of the building!"

Far below, screams once again pierced the air. Mup paused, staring downwards. There were several voices screaming at once down there. The dog must have found a group of people. Mup thought of the tailors weeping in their room. Of a group of washerwomen she had seen slumped over their tubs. The knots of helpless men and women she and Crow had passed in their headlong flight down through the many floors of the castle.

She could not tell if the screams she now heard were those of pain or fear. Were they the terrified sounds of people being chased . . . or something worse?

Mup resumed her frantic hammering on the window. "DAD!"

"I don't think this is your floor," cawed Crow.

"This is useless," cried Mup, slapping the glass. "We'll never find them!"

"Let's fly over."

Yes! Clever Crow! There were far fewer windows on the river side of the castle. And Mup could search directly for her bedroom, not just guess at corridor after endless corridor of black-and-white tiles. They shot upwards yet again, into the driving snow and wild breezes of the rooftops. Over the turrets and slopes they went, the countryside a great blanket of fog below, and then down again into the shelter of the riverside courtyard.

Mam was a vague huddle of white at the top of the boat steps, just another mound of snow in the featureless drifts of the yard.

"Wake up!" cried Mup from far above her. "Wake up!"

Oh, for grace," snarled Crow. He landed on the nearest snow-muffled windowsill, barely getting his footing before turning into a boy. Gathering snow in tight fistfuls, he hurled them at the motionless figure below.

"WAKE UP!" he shouted, slamming the snowballs hard into the yard. "IT DOESN'T MATTER IF YOU'RE SAD! JUST DO SOMETHING!"

Mup had time to see one of the snowballs explode, *pouf*, against Mam's shrouded figure before she turned to the windows, hunting for her room. *Here*, she thought, clinging like a spectre to the glass, looking down into the soft, pink comfort of her bed.

A sharp noise from the building below took her attention. Mup glanced down to see broken glass explode outwards in a glittering shower and tumble away to the ground. Someone had smashed a window from the inside. The glass was followed very quickly by Doctor Emberly, in his arms a fat and weeping chef. Emberly strained his way to the ground, safely deposited his heavy burden, and shot once again into the building.

Good Emberly, thought Mup. *Brave ghost.*

The sound of breaking glass came again from below, but Mup did not look anymore. Instead, she wrapped the belt of her dressing gown around her arm for protection, smashed her bedroom window with her elbow, and floated inside.

Her room was quiet and smelled of books and slippers. Mup floated down from the windowsill. She hovered above the floor, watchful for the sly crawl of drawings as she drifted to the door.

Dad had climbed onto a table. His tear-ravaged face strained and determined, he was holding Tipper high above his head, keeping him clear of the tide of drawings that swarmed the table's surface and stained Dad's trousers almost to the waist. Dad didn't even question Mup's appearance at her bedroom door. He just offered the iridescent bubble that held her brother. "Take him." Dad forced the words from gritted teeth. "Take him. All the blood's gone from my arms."

Mup took the burden from him. It wasn't heavy, but Dad must have been holding it up like that for hours. His arms flopped uselessly to his sides, and he doubled over on the tabletop, moaning in relief.

Mup peered through the bubble's shimmering surface at the twisted figure of her little brother. Tipper was still trapped in raven form. He had not moved since she'd seen him last. Mup hugged the bubble, as if by doing so she might also be hugging Tipper.

The little girl had done this to him. Why? To make him suffer the way others had suffered? To make Mup understand how others had suffered? If so, that wasn't fair. Tipper had never done anything to anyone. He was nothing but sunshine.

On the tabletop, Dad had struggled to his hands and knees. The drawings squirmed and nibbled at him. He swiped them away, and they just returned again with glee. "Let's . . . go . . . Mup," he said, sliding to the floor. The drawings followed him, a seething cloud swarming every surface he touched. But Dad—no longer using all his energy to hold up Tipper—somehow found the strength to stand. "Where is your mother?"

Mup glanced out of the window. Crow was down in the yard, fluttering and pecking at Mam's motionless figure. Mup could just about hear his nagging caws: *Move! Move! Use your magic! Be yourself!*

"Mam's on her way," she said.

Dad had already staggered to the door. The drawings dogged his every footstep, a heavy shadow he could not shake. Mup floated after him, Tipper in her arms. In the corridor, Dad slumped against the wall as Mup gazed towards the stairs, listening.

There were crashes and wails down there.

In the distance, another window smashed.

Mup thought she smelled smoke.

"Where are we going?" gasped Dad.

"I think we need to go upstairs, Dad. Can you manage that?"

He nodded. Mup led the way.

Halfway up the first flight of stairs, the ghost of Doctor Emberly startled them by bursting from the wainscotting, a terror of eyes and wild, dishevelled hair. "Oh, princess!" he yelled. "Thank grace I found you!" He gripped Mup in desperate hands, sending them both spinning in midair. "It's terrible down there!" he cried. "Terrible! The girl is smashing everything. She's setting things on fire!"

"Girl?" slurred Dad, slumping weakly against the banisters.

"Yes, sir. But all this destruction is just incidental." Emberly turned once more to Mup. "It's you the girl really wants, princess! You and your family. She and her dog are hunting you! You must run!"

Suddenly, the noises below them ceased, as if something down there had paused to listen.

Mup and Emberly froze. Mup held her breath.

"Oh dear," whispered Emberly. "I wonder if I may have inadvertently let her know where you are?"

As if in response, in the rooms far below, something howled in triumph.

A wild baying filled the air.

The noise began to work its way from floor to floor, heading upwards.

The Unbeatable Foe

"I don't understand!" gasped Mup, heaving Tipper up the last of the stairs and into the attic. "Why does she hate us? What have we ever done?"

"Perhaps you need not have done anything but be alive?" whispered Emberly, supporting Dad as he staggered behind her, a cloud of drawings trailing after him like a shadow.

They all froze as something shook the attic floorboards with a massive *boom*. Something not too far below fell and shattered. Much too close, the rage dog howled.

"Some people get like that," panted Dad, doggedly hauling himself forward despite the shadows clinging to his heels. "If the world hurts them badly enough. Other people's happiness comes to seem foolish to them, wicked even, an insult to all the terrible things they've been through. And they have to squash it or break it until everyone feels the way they do."

Mup looked down at the tortured figure of Tipper. Was that it? Was it precisely because he was so happy that she'd done this to him? Because he had been given the freedom to be himself and — being himself — had had the nerve to run and laugh and play in this terrible place where such terrible things had been done and witnessed?

"But that's not fair!" cried Mup.

"I know it's not," sighed Dad. "I know." He lay down on the floorboards. The drawings flooded in. "So tired," he whispered. "Just want to lie here and die."

Still floating carefully, Emberly squeezed Dad's arm. "I remember exactly how that feels," he said.

Mup punched open the skylight above their heads. She passed Tipper through and stooped to help Emberly lift Dad. "You're doing great, Dad. Just another bit to go."

"But then what?" Dad gasped, squeezing his massive shoulders through the little window. "Where do we go from here?"

Mup didn't know. She floated up onto the roof and looked around the wide, flat, wind-whipped expanse in which they now found themselves. Perilous drops surrounded them on all sides. *Perhaps I can contain the creature, like Naomi did?* she thought desperately. *Perhaps I can zap the grey girl?*

But Naomi hadn't been able to defeat either of them. What hope did Mup have?

I don't care, thought Mup fiercely. *I'll protect my family. I'll protect them with everything I've got.*

But how could she fight something made entirely of rage and memory? How could she fight something so deep-rooted and strong?

From the attic came a smashing, crunching, splintering noise, and then — directly below them — the relentless baying of an angry hound. Dad staggered to his feet. Emberly zoomed to support him. Mup snatched Tipper, and they retreated until they stood with their backs to a sheer drop — nowhere left to turn.

Snow and wind whipped them as the noises raged and rumbled below their feet. Then silence. There was a snuffling, searching moment as the hound investigated the opened skylight. Then, *boom,* its great, bristling head burst its way upwards. *Crash,* it shouldered its way through.

The hound oozed and slithered and writhed the rest of the way onto the roof. It seemed to have grown since the last time Mup saw it. Smoke followed it through the hole, and Mup realized that the dog's amorphous flesh was shot through with cracks of flame. Each giant, spreading paw left smouldering footprints in its wake.

The grey girl rose into the air behind it, floating up through the jagged remains of the shattered window frame. She had changed from the mouselike creature Mup had previously known. She was upright and righteous now, rising from the shadows. Her round eyes had grown to almost fill her triangular face. Snow became fiery embers as it blew through her thin body.

The girl's dog paced before her, howling — waiting for permission to attack.

"Listen!" cried Mup.

"No," said the girl. She jerked her hand and the dog lunged.

"Nooo!" cried Mup. Without thinking, she threw Tipper to Emberly and aimed all her power at the dog. Lightning shook her hands. It traced an arc of steam through the falling snow and hit the dog in mid-leap. The dog flew one way, Mup the other. All was a confusion of upflung snow as she landed on her back and slid to the edge of the roof. Then she was out in midair, the wind a breathless rush around her. She fell like a stone, her heart left behind.

Then she gritted her teeth and flew.

Far below, she heard cawing. A dull shape was dragging itself across the yard. But there was no time to see more. Mup shot back to the rooftop.

The little grey girl was standing with her back to Mup, one arm out, straining. A wide, smoking track stretched away from her—the path that had been cleared by the rage dog as it slid over the far edge of the roof. Dad and Emberly were watching the girl with wide eyes, Tipper clutched protectively in the ghost's transparent arms. Mup shot across to them.

The little girl raised her outstretched arm. It was a struggle for her, as if she were lifting a heavy weight. Her trembling arm rose, and her dog floated into view. Huge and struggling and obviously afraid, it paddled the air with burning feet.

"Let's go," whispered Mup, taking Dad under the arm. "While she's distracted."

"Go *where?*" insisted Emberly.

Gently, the grey girl placed the huge monster back on the roof. She stroked it tenderly, embers flaring under her dull hand. Then she pointed to her huddled prey.

"Fetch," she said.

"No!" cried Emberly.

The dog leapt. Emberly dropped Tipper and ran.

Mup had a moment to think, *You coward!* Then she stepped between the leaping dog and her family. She spread her arms and tensed her body. She did this without thinking, in the same instinctive way you hold your breath when you fall in deep water.

She spread her arms, she tensed her body, and the dog came to a halt in mid-leap.

Mup instantly regretted not shooting lightning. She was now trapped with this terrible pressure on her — the exact same feeling as if she were holding her breath. The dog was suspended right above her, jaws open, eyes flaming, great claws spread. Mup was all there was between it and Dad and Tipper, and she knew she wasn't going to be able to hold it.

Doctor Emberly ducked under the belly of the beast. He was heading for the attic window, running away. If Mup had had the breath, she would have cursed him.

But Doctor Emberly did not run for the window. He ran straight for the grey girl.

"Miss," he said. "Miss, please. What good is all this destruction? What possible use is it to those of us who've suffered?"

The girl, her eyes fixed on Mup, just stalked right through him — ghost through ghost — as if he weren't there. Doctor Emberly jerked. He screamed. The little

185

girl's darkness swirled outwards, filling him like ash in a teardrop. She came out the other side, and, shuddering, Doctor Emberly fell to the snow. The grey girl walked away and left him to his struggles, her darkness having stolen all his light.

Mup sank to her knees, straining as she held the dog at bay. From the corner of her eye, she could see Tipper slowly rolling to the edge of the roof. Dad, painfully hampered by shadows, was crawling after him.

The grey girl bent to look into Mup's sweating face. "But of course," she rasped. "You protect the ones you love." She gestured to the smoke pouring from the attics below. "All those others were not important enough for you to help."

"What?" cried Mup. "No! That's not . . ."

Behind her, Tipper rolled off the roof.

Dad bellowed in despair. Mup turned, screaming for her brother.

The dog—released by her distraction—let loose a howl and completed its leap across her head. It bit the place where Dad had been. Flaming splinters scattered from its maw as it tore a huge chunk from the roof. It did not take long for the dog to realize that its prey was missing, and it whined in frustration, snuffling around for Dad's scent.

Dad had scrambled desperately, and far too late, to the place where Tipper had rolled over the edge. He clung perilously to the gutter, drawings writhing all around him in the snow, and gazed down after his son.

Snarling, the rage dog advanced on him.

Mup scrambled to her feet. Her heart mourned. *Tipper, Tipper.* But there was no time to stop. She took all her anger and all her fear and fired it at the dog.

The dog flinched, and nothing more. It turned its face to Mup. She fired again. The dog roared a reply, and its hot ashy blast toppled Mup onto her back and sent her skidding past the solemnly observant little girl. She slammed against a chimney stack in an explosion of snow.

There was a moment of calm while the grey girl and her dog watched Mup climb painfully to her feet. Within that brief quiet, a sound rose up from where Tipper had fallen. A sound so sweet that Mup and the dog and the girl all turned to look in its direction.

A raven rose to sight, sailing up past the edge of the roof, its wings spread against a buffeting updraught. It was Crow. His round eyes were fixed on something below. His beak was open in a song of unspeakable purity and grace.

Below him rose Tipper—still trapped within his

iridescent bubble—carried upwards through the driving snow by Crow's beautiful song.

A familiar arm slapped up and over the edge of the roof. Dark and crawling with drawings, as if tattooed by them, it groped for purchase on the snow-slicked gutter. Dad reached much too far over the edge, grabbed, and heaved back, hauling Mam into sight.

She crawled the rest of the way, surrounded by shadows. Too held down by them to fly, she had scaled the building to protect her own. Snarling with effort, Dad jerked to his knees and helped Mam to stand. Defying the darkness that swarmed them both, they clung together, tottering at the edge of the drop. Mam lifted her hand and blasted the dog with everything she had.

The dog reared, howling.

Mup fired too—short, sharp blasts to boost Mam's prolonged ones.

The dog writhed.

Yes, thought Mup, triumphantly blasting lightning into the animal's form. *Yes! We can do this. We could beat this thing. Maybe sometimes you have to be a weapon.*

She and Mam continued firing, channelling all their energy into lightning and fire. Under the barrage of combined power, the dog roared and snarled and popped. It reared up high, high, high on its smouldering back legs, then slammed down hard on all four paws. It roared its fiery roar.

Mup stopped shooting.

The dog had gotten bigger.

Mam too paused, obviously realizing the truth.

Every shot was helping the creature grow. Every shot was making it stronger.

Mam and Mup looked at each other, understanding that they could not win.

Then the dog leapt again, snarling, and Mam had no choice but to shoot it — driving it momentarily back as she and Dad began to edge away. The dog bounced forward, swiping at them, almost puppyish in its violent playfulness. A trail of smouldering footsteps marked its progress across the roof.

Mup raced to the little girl, frustration burning her spine, crackling in her hands.

"Why are you doing this?" she screamed.

The girl expanded with rage. She roared: "YOU HAVE NO RIGHT TO BE HAPPY!"

These booming words jarred the roof beams, throwing Mup into the air. Mup landed with a *bam*, immediately rolled to her knees, and slapped the ground furiously. "YOU'RE HURTING PEOPLE YOU DON'T EVEN KNOW!"

A shockwave of power slammed from Mup's hand, flinging snow and girl and dog backwards. The grey girl tumbled head over heels, coming to a rest by Doctor Emberly. The poor doctor lay shivering and moaning, wreathed in the smoke that poured from the broken attic window. Ignoring him, the grey girl clambered to her hands and knees, glaring at Mup.

"Yooou forrrgot us!"

"No!"

"Yeeeeessss!" hissed the girl, crawling like a vengeful spider through the smoke and snow. "You *wiped* us." She gestured with her arm, a broad movement as if cleaning a window. "You *wiped us out.*"

"Wiped . . . ?" Mup recoiled, remembering the ash on her hands, her frantic destruction of the girl's drawings. Those drawings—those *names*—the only remaining trace of people thrown away and forgotten. The girl had spent decades, maybe even centuries, saving them and Mup had erased them in a moment. "They were hurting Crow," she whispered.

The girl gripped her own chest, her face a twist of agony. "Yes," she moaned. "They hurt." She curled around herself, a little girl again, crouched in smoke and ashes, her pain strong enough to distract even her great rage.

Mup almost reached for her. The girl was so small suddenly and so overcome. Mup wanted to say to her, *I'm sorry you hurt.* But the girl snarled and slammed her hand down and glared up once again in fiery rage, and Mup realized she didn't know how to fix her. All those horrible memories, all those terrible things the girl had seen and suffered—they were too much to even look at.

I don't want to look at them, thought Mup. *I shouldn't have to look at them. They're nothing to do with me.* She didn't want to feel that way. But she did. Even now, Mup had to admit that it would be so much easier, so much less painful and complicated, if she could just wipe this girl away, as she'd wiped away her drawings, and never have to think about her again.

Mam and Dad were still backing painfully away from the rage dog, Mam barely holding it at bay with weaker and weaker bolts of lightning. It padded after them, every footstep spreading fire—the last living trace of countless abused and discarded people. Mup supposed some of those people might have been happy once, perhaps gentle and funny and kind, but now they were just this—this monster of rage and pain, the only memory the little girl had been able to save of them.

"You . . . will . . . *forget* . . . us," rasped the girl.

And she was right. These people would be forgotten—they had *already* been forgotten—by everyone but her. "But this is not remembering," whispered Mup, watching the rage dog once again bite the ground. She turned urgently. The girl flinched as Mup grabbed her hand. "This is not remembering! This will do nothing but destroy people—good people, bad people, everyone. It'll turn everything to ash until there's no one left at all."

The girl tried to pull away, but Mup held on.

"Look at poor Emberly," she cried. "Look what you've done to him."

Emberly groaned and muttered, his eyes all black with remembered pain. The girl stared at him, as if only now realizing who he was. "Errr-asss-musss?" she asked.

"Yes! Look what you've done to Erasmus! He's only just escaped the dark, and you've put him right back in it again."

"Errasmusss . . . escaped . . . ?"

"Yes! And look at poor Tipper!" Mup gestured at her little brother, trapped and twisted in the witch's bubble. "He's just brand-new! He's brand-new and shiny and you've hurt him! Why? What good can it do to hurt a happy little person like Tip?"

192

The girl sat back. She seemed to look for the first time at the world around her: the destruction, the smoke, the fire. She looked again at Emberly, poor Emberly, tortured once more with the pain and darkness he had only just escaped, and she seemed to sag a little.

"It doesn't have to be like this," whispered Mup. "You don't have to hurt everyone just to make them understand how you feel."

The girl searched Mup's eyes, centuries of wariness behind her hesitation.

"We can find another way to make people remember," said Mup. "Help me find another way. I promise, I will never let anyone forget."

"What . . . what is your name, witch?"

"My name is Mup. What's yours?"

The girl tilted her ashy head, as if not understanding the question.

"Don't you have a name?"

"I have many," said the girl.

Gently, she pulled her hand from Mup's. She got to her feet and turned away.

First, the girl touched Emberly. The ash swirling inside him changed course as if drawn to the girl's hand. It channelled up through her arm; it seemed to enter her heart. The girl grew darker, but Emberly

193

brightened. He relaxed, sighing, into the snow, and the pain went from his eyes.

Next, the girl went to Tipper, who still hung suspended by Crow's song above the roof. She pressed a finger to the bubble's surface. The agonized shape inside popped and untwisted. The raven became a dog. Crow cawed in panic as the weight became too much for his song to carry. Tipper plopped to the ground, a sweet, fat Labrador puppy, fast asleep in a shiny bubble.

The grey girl peered at him, as if trying to understand. "Happy," she whispered.

Next, she went to her dog.

Mup ran with her, putting herself between the girl and Mam. "Stop shooting!" she yelled. "Mam! Stop shooting!"

At Mup's shout, Mam paused her rapid blasts of lightning. She and Dad were barely keeping their feet, drawings swarming them like flies. The little grey girl regarded them curiously as she passed. It was as if she'd never seen them before. Mup wondered what it was she'd been seeing all this time. Who she thought she'd been hunting? Raggedy witches, perhaps? Her old tormentors?

The rage dog prowled and whined in confusion as the girl reached for its bristling head.

"Shhh," she said. She stroked its flaming muzzle. "Shhh."

At her touch, the dog sighed. It closed its eyes. Contented, it lay down at the girl's feet. The girl continued to stroke its ears, its neck, its powerful back. The dog nuzzled her hand.

Soon, it was no bigger than a large puppy.

Soon, it was not there at all.

The girl rose from where she had been crouching in the snow. She turned to Mup. She had not yet lost her frowning, wary look.

Mup nodded to her: *I promise. I will never let you down.*

The girl sighed. She seemed tired now, a weariness of centuries, which she could never sleep off. She lifted her face to the falling snow as if for one last time. Mup felt unbearably sorry for her. She was so sad, and so lonely. It would never be any different for her because she carried too much pain.

The little grey girl crouched once more. She pressed her hand to the smoky ground. Darkness swarmed her from every corner — all the shadows she had sent out into the world. They scuttled home, a seemingly endless tide of them, and the little grey girl absorbed them all. Soon her fire was dead, the snow passing through her was just ash; she was as dark as she had ever been. Even darker perhaps, because she'd added to her burden with the suffering she'd just caused: more names to remember, more pain for her to carry on and on.

She climbed wearily to her feet. She looked one more time at Mup.

"Do not forget," she said—and she was gone.

Calls in the Fog

They sat on the rooftop, too weary yet to move. Emberly sprawled, silent and alone on the far side of the roof, as if needing space to think. The rest of them huddled together with their backs to the shelter of the parapet. The snow fell and fell and fell all around them. They ignored it.

"I wonder what's on fire in there," murmured Dad as they all watched the smoke pouring from various holes and cracks to snatch away in the wind.

"Can't be too big a fire," muttered Crow, huddling closer. "This roof's not even slightly warm under my bum."

Dad put his arm around him and leaned his head back, closing his eyes.

"We'll climb down in a minute," said Mam. Her eyes too were closed; she was leaning against Dad.

Tipper was on her lap, a baby for once, only his head and his little feet visible from where Mam had zipped him up inside her jacket.

Mam had popped Naomi's bubble with one finger. Tipper had plopped out onto the snow. He had woken long enough to mumble "Mammy." Then he'd rolled over, turned into a baby, and promptly fallen back asleep.

He'll be a puppy again tomorrow, thought Mup. For now, he just wanted a cuddle.

She climbed tiredly to her feet and spread her hands on the parapet.

"Y'OK, Mup?" asked Mam, briefly opening her eyes.

Mup nodded, listening to the stones.

Mam sighed. "I need to get down there and see what the damage is." She didn't move.

But that was OK. Mup knew that whatever waited for them downstairs—awful and all as it might be—the worst was over. The castle felt calm and whole again. It felt healed. Somewhere down there, the little grey girl still haunted the shadows, but there was a patience to her presence now. Mup had made her a promise. The girl knew she'd keep it. She was willing to wait.

Up here, though . . . Mup lifted her gaze to take in the countryside. Up here, the world was still a drifting landscape of white. Her grandmother's curse still held the castle firmly in its grip. *We're alone,* thought Mup. *We're alone, because everyone believes there's no other choice but to be alone.*

She was turning to say this to her mam when a movement in the fog caught her eye.

Out in the distance, where the far bank of the river should have been visible, it came again: a brief flurry of dark. Had she imagined it? By Dad's side, Crow stirred, listening.

"*By . . . by the rim of my tall hat,*" he whispered,
"*Can nobody but me hear that?*"

He climbed to his feet by Mup's side, listening with all his might.

"There!" cried Mup. "Out there! In the fog!"

She pointed excitedly to another flurry of movement.

A tiny speck flapped towards them through the muffling air.

Crow flung back his head and cawed. A chorus of voices answered from the fog.

"Yippeee!" Crow pranced in uncontained glee around the smoking roof. He cawed and danced, and danced and cawed. Mam and Dad smiled tiredly at him while, out in the fog, Crow's people returned his call.

The speck of grey grew to a misty shape: bright eyes, spread wings, noble beak—a massive silver raven. It sailed over Mup's grinning head and wheeled down to land on the splintered roof. Mam rose to greet it, Tipper's sleeping weight cradled in her jacket, Dad smiling by her side.

"Fírinne," she said.

The silver raven hopped once, twice. It shook its massive wings. On the third hop, it became a woman. "By grace," panted Fírinne, shaking frost from her shining hair. "After a lifetime of being a cat, that feels very strange." She winked at Dad. "Can't say I didn't enjoy it, though."

Mam stepped forward, wordless, and squeezed her friend's arm.

Around Mup, the parapets echoed with the call of ravens. Wings agitated the air. Birds landed, and in their place rose the women and men of Clann'n Cheoil.

"But the curse!" Mup laughed. "The snow!"

Fírinne leaned down to her. "You were right," she whispered. "It's only snow. It made things difficult—but not impossible. All we had to do was try harder." She kissed Mup on her forehead. "Let your grandmother try her worst," she said. "Let her send snow and fog and rain and whatever elemental misfortunes as she may. Let her spy on us through the moon and lurk with her minions at the edges of our world. We still have our voices. We still have our hands and feet. We will not stop working for a better world until we're dead and in the grave."

"Not even then," said Emberly quietly from his position by the far wall.

"Not even then," agreed Fírinne, fiercely.

She turned, bright-eyed, to Mam. Whatever she had been going to say died on her lips as she looked around her for the first time. "Good grace," she said, taking in the roiling smoke, the scorched and splintered roof. "I've been gone less than a day . . . What have you savages done to the place?"

Remember

"I do not understand," muttered the butler, "why Her Majesty felt the need to put that grace-blasted thing there."

"I agree," sighed his associate. "Couldn't she have put it somewhere less obvious? Somewhere more discreet? There's no way in and out other than up those boat steps and through this yard. One can't help but see it. Who wants to be confronted by that every time they come and go from the castle?"

They passed Mup in the doorway of the guardroom, bowing curtly and tucking their empty trays behind their backs. Mup watched them mutter their way back into the gloom of the downstairs passageways. She wound a scarf around her neck, pulled on her Wellingtons, and stepped outside.

It was still snowing. It had been for weeks. But that was all right. It was just snow. It fell, and people dug it out. It fell again, and they dug it out again. They helped each other stay warm; they helped each other stay alive—and that was all that was needed for now.

Fírinne was lounging just outside the door with the men and women of *Clann'n Cheoil*, eating the lunch that the butlers had just provided them. They would get back to work soon, their voices raised, their eyes lifted, as their subtle melodies manoeuvred heavy blocks through the snowy air and slotted them carefully into place, rebuilding the defences of the river wall.

"Your father is still at this madness with Crow," said Fírinne to Mup, indicating the boat steps, where Dad and Crow huddled together, their heads bent over a set of plans that they'd carefully spread out on the stones between them.

Mup grinned. "It'll work out, Fírinne. Just wait and see."

Fírinne tsked grouchily, and Mup grinned wider and pulled on her rabbit-eared hat.

Dad's and Crow's faces were creased in identical concentration as they bent over their diagrams, scribbling and calculating and muttering things like *Ah-ha* and *Oh-ho!*

They'd been drawing this plan for weeks. Today was the day they started work.

A whistle drifted up from the river, and Crow looked up excitedly.

"They're here!" he cried. "Look! Look!"

Fírinne shook her head in bemusement as the first of many brightly painted, splintered pieces of wood were carried into sight up the boat steps. "Where shall you even put it?" she called to Dad.

"Wherever Crow fancies," he answered. "It's his home, after all."

"It's hardly more than a pile of tinder."

"Nothing a hammer and a few nails won't fix," called Crow cheerfully.

"A hammer," agreed Dad as the great battered, bowed roof of Crow's *cáirín* was carried into sight. "A few nails. And maybe a bit of magic. Right, Crow?"

Sighing, Fírinne shook her head and strode down to help with the unloading.

Her people got to their feet and went back to work.

Behind Mup, further back in the courtyard, Mam laughed and Tipper barked, both of them deeply invested in their game. Mam always took lunchtime off. Even though so many people came to see her now, and she was nearly always busy, she always spent lunchtime throwing a Frisbee with Tipper in the snow.

Before turning around to look at her mam and her brother, Mup took a deep breath, trying to prepare herself. She knew they were playing down by the wall. And it was always best to prepare yourself for the wall. Steeling herself, Mup turned and the sadness struck her with just as much force as the first time she'd seen it. Perhaps it would always be like this, this first huge blast of sadness. If so, that was all right. It took nothing from her — this tiny moment in the midst of her happy day, this tiny moment of remembrance and respect.

Mam and Tipper, dwarfed by the wall's immensity, played on as if in happy disregard of it. But Mup knew that Mam would have had to take a similar moment when confronted by it. She would have had to stop and look up, and for a moment, the wall would have overwhelmed her with its rows upon rows of endlessly scrolling lists of names. Mam would have had no choice but to acknowledge it, as everyone who ever passed through the yard had to do, before going on with her work or play.

Tipper did not even seem to see it. The wall looked just the same to him as all the other walls of the yard. Mam said it was because he was too young. She said, one day, when Tipper was old enough to understand, he would look up and he would stop like everyone else. The names would be visible to him on that day, and from that day on he would never forget them. From that day on Tipper would stop like everyone else on first coming into the yard, and he would pause, his eyes would fill with tears, and he would remember before going on with his day.

But not now. Not yet. For now, Tipper was still too young.

Tipper jerked his head and flung the Frisbee particularly hard.

Mam shot into the air and caught it before it could sail off into the river.

"Not fair!" barked Tipper. "No flying!"

Mam laughed breathlessly. "You have four legs! I have to have *some* advantage."

Badger, tucked up nice and warm in a little pile of rugs, licked Mup's hand as she passed by. She bent and patted his grizzled head before heading on to the wall.

"Hello, Doctor Emberly," she said, joining the ghost in his perusal of the endlessly scrolling lists. The ghost just *hmmed* at her and continued his shortsighted reading, his nose almost brushing the wall. Mup shuffled her feet. "Doctor Emberly," she said. "You know, you've been staring at that wall day and night for such a long time now. Ever since the girl's lists first appeared there. I wonder if it might do you some good to do something else for a while?"

"Mmmhmm," said Emberly, moving on to another section.

"It's just . . ." Mup hurried to catch up as he moved on down the rows. "Doctor Emberly, it's just that you spent so long in the dark. I hate to see you not having fun now that you finally have a chance."

"Yes," murmured Doctor Emberly. "In the dark."

Mup gently took his arm. "Doctor Emberly, don't you want to do something else now?"

He turned to look in Mup's face, surprising her with his unexpected severity. "She's not on the list," he said.

"Pardon?"

"Everyone else is here. Look. There's me." He poked the wall in exasperation, his finger travelling upwards until his name scrolled out of reach. "There's Crow's father. Even, look, the poor folks that dog killed." Emberly paused, drumming his fingers on the wall. "But she's not here," he muttered. "I'm certain now. She's nowhere on these lists." He turned suddenly and tramped off through the snow.

Mup raced after him. "Doctor Emberly . . . ?"

"I can't tolerate it," he said. "Not even for her . . ."

He disappeared into the tunnels. Mup hesitated only a moment, then followed suit.

They quickly left the snowy light and singing, the sounds of laughter behind. Mup wasn't frightened. It was dark in here, and cold, but that was all. The grey girl was at peace. Her dog was laid to rest. There was nothing in these tunnels now but sadness, and a little damp running down the walls. Mup raised her hand to light the way.

She followed Emberly down and down the familiar sloping path. Down past the cells, breathing their loneliness into the dark. Past the blank-walled tunnel. Down, at last, the spiralled corridor to the oubliette.

A dim light glimmered there, around the final bend.

Mup knew, before she even saw her, who the ghost would be.

Naomi looked up as they rounded the corner. Faint and dimly shimmering, she was sitting on a pile of rubble next to the heap of torn black cloth that was all that remained of her living form. Mup noted that no one had yet been down here to claim the piles of ancient bones.

Emberly bent to Naomi, who regarded him a little slackly, as if waking from a dream.

"Poor thing," he said. "Things are a mite confusing, aren't they? After one dies? Do you even know where you are?"

Naomi blinked at him. "I . . . I'm in the dark," she whispered. "It's no more than I deserve."

"Hmmhmm," said Emberly. "Well, that's as may be." He took Naomi's luminous hand. "But let's try something different, shall we? Let's try something new."

He pulled Naomi to her feet. Mup gently took her other hand.

Between them, Mup and Emberly led the witch into the light.

Before the castle, before the snow,
Mup had to cross from our world
into Witches Borough . . .

★ "Kiernan has crafted something at once familiar and delightfully surprising with this fantasy quest." —*Kirkus Reviews* (starred review)

"Kiernan finds magic in music, rhyme, and freedom of speech in this brilliant adventure into another world." —*Booklist*

Available in hardcover, paperback, and audio and as an e-book

www.candlewick.com

Look for the riveting conclusion to the Wild Magic trilogy!

Witches Borough has gone from smothering blizzard to parching drought. Into the scorched landscape storms a raggedy witch, trailing ashes in her wake: Magda, Crow's mother. She wants Mup to fulfill a promise. She wants Mup to help her.

Available in hardcover and as an e-book

Turn the page for an excerpt. . . .

A Rebel School for Rebel Children

Mup smiled as she stepped into the classroom. She had helped Mam choose this room. Desks and chairs waited patiently for new occupants. Bookcases were ripe with untold adventure. A row of glasses twinkled next to jugs of water, in case the children were thirsty after their long walk to school. Bright, airy windows and a stained-glass door opened onto the courtyard garden from which Mup and Crow had just entered. The children would be able to run around this garden if they liked, or fly among the trees, or nestle in the mud at the bottom of the tiny pond that, before the drought, had brightened the centre of the lawn.

"Whatever the students need to learn, let them learn it," Mam had told the teachers. "Whatever they need to become, let them become it."

Mup wiggled her toes in one of the bright splashes

of colour that the stained glass threw across the floor. *It's perfect*, she thought. *They're going to love it.*

On the opposite side of the room, a door led to an interior corridor, which led to a flight of steps, which led to the old guardroom, which opened onto the riverside courtyard.

Tipper's voice echoed happily from the shadows there. "This way, childrens! Follow me!"

With a skitter of claws and a merry bark, Mup's little brother bounded into the room. All fat paws, all waving tail, all jolly golden face, he lolloped merrily around the desks, barked, "Hello, Crow! Hello, Mup! Hello, hello!" and bounced right back out again.

Grinning, Mup ran after him to wait in the doorway. The new students were edging down the steps and into the corridor. They were a row of owlish faces in the gloom. The light of the riverside courtyard seeped in from the cloakroom behind them. Fírinne was a tall shape within the door there, standing guard. Mup waved up to her. Fírinne raised a hand in reply.

Dad's distinctive, broad-shouldered silhouette joined the tall, slim *clann* leader. Fírinne leaned on one side of the door frame, her arms crossed, Dad leaned on the other, and the two of them began talking in low voices. Mup knew they were discussing the safety of

An excerpt from The Promise Witch

these children, the possibility of Mup's grandmother engineering some kind of vengeance against their parents.

Crow came to Mup's side, and the approaching children eyed the two of them cautiously.

Mup beamed at them and flung her arms wide. "Welcome to Magic School!"

Unsmiling, the silent children crept past and into the classroom.

"It'll be OK," Mup said gently. "It'll be OK. I promise."

Tipper bounded about, excitedly barking. He snuffled pockets and licked tentatively reaching hands. The children began to smile. They began to look around the sunny room. *Whatever they'd expected,* Mup thought, *it can't have been this bright, happy, noisy place.*

"Fírinne!" barked Tipper, running to the school-room door. "Fírinne, where is Badger? You said you'd help him down the stairs!"

Fírinne's voice rose up in the guardroom and all the children laughed as Mup's dear old grey-faced Labrador, Badger, floated down the corridor, into the room, and was deposited gently by the door. Delighted with himself, Badger strolled from child to enchanted child, stiffly wagging his tail and introducing himself with polite licks on their outstretched hands.

An excerpt from The Promise Witch

Crow began solemnly handing out notebooks and pens, a name badge for each pupil.

Tipper noticed a tiny girl lurking at the door. "Come in! Come in!" he barked.

The little girl just stared.

Mup went to her. "No need to be scared," she whispered. "No one will hurt you."

The little girl seemed to doubt this. "Not even Teacher?" she asked.

At the word "teacher," the other children went silent. They seemed to withdraw.

"Will . . . will Teacher be here soon?" asked one of the boys.

"Teacher's *already* here," grunted Crow with his usual lack of tact.

The children gasped. Their eyes darted to the big desk at the front of the room.

The sunlight streaming in the windows there had made it easy to miss the ghost. To a passing glance, she could be mistaken for just a shadow. But once you knew she was there, there was no missing her, and once you'd seen her, there was no mistaking the tall, dark-clad spectre for anything other than what she was— a raggedy witch.

An excerpt from The Promise Witch